Capt'n Davy's Honeymoon

Capt'n Davy's Honeymoon

Hall Caine

MINT EDITIONS

Capt'n Davy's Honeymoon was first published in 1892.

This edition published by Mint Editions 2020.

ISBN 9781513267647 | E-ISBN 9781513272641

Published by Mint Editions®

MINT
EDITIONS
minteditionbooks.com

Publishing Director: Jennifer Newens
Design & Production: Rachel Lopez Metzger
Typesetting: Westchester Publishing Services

I

"M y money, ma'am—my money, not me."

"So you say, sir."

"It's my money you've been marrying, ma'am."

"Maybe so, sir."

"Deny it, deny it!"

"Why should I? You say it is so, and so be it."

"Then d——— the money. It took me more till ten years to make it, and middling hard work at that; but you go bail it'll take me less nor ten months to spend it. Ay, or ten weeks, and aisy doing, too! And 'till it's gone, Mistress Quig-gin—d'ye hear me?—gone, every mortal penny of it gone, pitched into the sea, scattered to smithereens, blown to ould Harry, and dang him—I'll lave ye, ma'am, I'll lave ye; and, sink or swim, I'll darken your doors no more."

The lady and gentleman who blazed at each other with these burning words, which were pointed, and driven home by flashing eyes and quivering lips, were newly-married husband and wife. They were staying at the old Castle Mona, in Douglas, Isle of Man, and their honeymoon had not yet finished its second quarter. The gentleman was Captain Davy Quiggin, commonly called Capt'n Davy, a typical Manx sea-dog, thirty years of age; stalwart, stout, shaggy, lusty-lunged, with the tongue of a trooper, the heavy manners of a bear, the stubborn head of a stupid donkey, and the big, soft heart of the baby of a girl. The lady was Ellen Kinvig, known of old to all and sundry as Nelly, Ness, or Nell, but now to everybody concerned as Mistress Capt'n Davy Quiggin, six-and-twenty years of age, tall, comely, as blooming as the gorse; once as free as the air, and as racy of the soil as new-cut peat, but suddenly grown stately, smooth, refined, proud, and reserved. They loved each other to the point of idolatry; and yet they parted ten days after marriage with these words of wroth and madness. Something had come between them. What was it? Another man? No. Another woman? Still no. What then? A ghost, an intangible, almost an invisible but very real and divorce-making co-respondent. They call it Education.

Davy Quiggin was born in a mud house on the shore, near the old church at Ballaugh. The house had one room only, and it had been the living-room, sleeping-room, birth-room, and death-room of a family of six. Davy, who was the youngest, saw them all out. The last to go were his mother and his grandfather. They lay ill at the same time, and died on the one day. The old man died first, and Davy fixed up a herring-net in front of him, where he lay on the settle by the fire, so that his mother might not see him from her place on the bed.

Not long after that, Davy, who was fifteen years of age, went to live as farm lad with Kinvig, of Ballavolley. Kinvig was a solemn person, very stiff and starchy, and sententious in his way, a mighty man among the Methodists, and a power in the pulpit. He thought he had done an act of charity when he took Davy into his home, and Davy repaid him in due time by falling in love with Nelly, his daughter.

When that happened Davy never quite knew. "That's the way of it," he used to say. "A girl slips in, and there ye are." Nelly was in to a certainty when one night Davy came home late from the club meeting on the street, and rapped at the kitchen window. That was the signal of the home circle that some member of it was waiting at the door. Now there are ways and ways of rapping at a kitchen window. There is the pit-a-pat of a light heart, and the thud-thud of a heavy one; and there is the sharp crack-crack of haste, and the dithering que-we-we of fear. Davy had a rap of his own, and Nelly knew it.

There was a sort of a trip and dance and a rum-tum-tum in Davy's rap that always made Nelly's heart and feet leap up at the same instant. But on this unlucky night it was Nelly's mother who heard it, and opened the door. What happened then was like the dismal sneck of the outside gate to Davy for ten years thereafter. The porch was dark, and so was the little square lobby behind the door. On numerous other nights that had been an advantage in Davy's eyes, but on this occasion he thought it a snare of the evil one. Seeing something white in a petticoat he threw his arms about it and kissed and hugged it madly. It struck him at the time as strange that the arms he held did not clout him under the chin, and that the lips he smothered did not catch breath enough to call him a gawbie, and whisper that the old people inside were listening. The truth dawned on him in a moment, and then he felt like a man with an eel crawling down his back, and he wanted nothing else for supper.

It was summer time, and Davy, though a most accomplished sleeper, found no difficulty in wakening himself with the dawn next morning. He was cutting turf in the dubs of the Curragh just then, and he had four hours of this pastime, with spells of sober meditation between, before he came up to the house for breakfast. Then as he rolled in at the porch, and stamped the water out of his long-legged boots, he saw at a glance that a thunder-cloud was brewing there. Nelly was busy at the long table before the window, laying the bowls of milk and the deep plates for the porridge. Her print frock was as sweet as the May blossom, her cheeks were nearly as red as the red rose, and like the rose her head hung down. She did not look at him as he entered. Neither did Mrs. Kinvig, who was bending over the pot swung from the hook above the fire, and working the porridge-stick round and round with unwonted energy. But Kinvig himself made up for both of them. The big man was shaving before a looking-glass propped up on the table, and against the Pilgrim's Progress and Clark's Commentaries. His left hand held the point of his nose aside between the tip of his thumb and first finger, while the other swept the razor through a hillock of lather and revealed a portion of a mouth twisted three-quarters across his face. But the moment he saw Davy he dropped the razor, and looked up with as much dignity as a man could get out of a countenance half covered with soap.

"Come in, sir," said he, with a pretense of great deference. "Mawther," he said, twisting to Mrs. Kinvig, "just wipe down a chair for the gentleman."

Davy slithered into his seat. "I'm in for it," he thought.

"They're telling me," said Kinvig, "that there is a fortune coming at you. Aw, yes, though, and that you're taking notions on a farmer's girl. Respectable man, too—one of the first that's going, with sixty acres at him and more. Amazing thick, they're telling me. Kissing behind the door, and the like of that! The capers! It was only yesterday you came to me with nothing on your back but your father's ould trowis, cut down at the knees."

Nelly slipped out. Her mother made a noise with the porridge-pot. Davy was silent. Kinvig walloped his razor on the strop with terrific vigor, then paused, pointed the handle in Davy's direction, tried to curl up his lip into a withering sneer that was half lost in the lather, and said with bitter irony, "My house is too mane for you, sir. You must lave me. It isn't the Isle of Man itself that'll hould the likes of you."

Then Davy found his tongue. "You're right, sir," said he, leaping to his feet, "It's too poor I am for your daughter, is it? Maybe I'll be a piece richer someday, and then you'll be a taste civiler."

"Behold ye now," said Kinvig, "as bould as a goat! Cut your stick and quick."

"I'm off, sir," said Davy; and, then, looking round and remembering that he was being kicked out like a dog and would see Nelly no more, day by day, the devil took hold of him and he began to laugh in Kinvig's ridiculous face.

"Good-by, ould Sukee," he cried. "I lave you to your texes."

And, turning to where Mrs. Kinvig stood with her back to him, he cried again, "Good-by, mawther, take care of his ould head—it's swelling so much that his chapel hat is putting corns on it."

That night with his "chiss" of clothes on his shoulders, Davy came down stairs and went out at the porch. There he slipped his burden to the ground, for somebody was waiting to say farewell to him. It was the right petticoat this time, and she was on the right side of the door. The stars were shining overhead, but two that were better than any in the sky were looking into Davy's face, and they were twinkling in tears.

It was only a moment the parting lasted, but a world of love was got into it. Davy had to do penance for the insults he had heaped upon Nelly's father, and in return he got pity for those that had been shoveled upon himself.

"Good-by, Nell," he whispered; "there's thistles in everybody's crop. But no matter! I'll come back, and then it's married we'll be. My goodness, yes, and take Ballacry and have six bas'es, and ten pigs, and a pony. But, Nelly, will ye wait for me?"

"D'ye doubt me, Davy?"

"No; but will ye though?"

"Yes."

"Then its all serene," said Davy, and with another hug and a kiss, and a lock of brown hair which was cut ready and tied in blue ribbon, he was gone with his chest into the darkness.

Davy sailed in an Irish schooner to the Pacific coast of South America. There he cut his stick again, and got a berth on a coasting steamer trading between Valparaiso and Callao. The climate was unhealthy, the ports were foul, the government was uncertain, the dangers were constant, and the hands above him dropped off rapidly. In two years Davy was skipper, and in three years more he was sailing a steamer of his own. Then the money began to tumble into his chest like crushed oats out of a Crown's shaft.

The first hundred pounds he had saved he sent home to Dumbell's bank, because he could not trust it out of the Isle of Man. But the hundreds grew to thousands, and the thousands to tens of thousands, and to send all his savings over the sea as he made them began to be slow work, like supping porridge with a pitchfork. He put much of it away in paper rolls at the bottom of his chest in the cabin, and every roll he put by stood to him for something in the Isle of Man. "That's a new cowhouse at Ballavolly." "That's Balladry." "That's ould Brew's mill at Sulby—he'll be out by this time."

All his dreams were of coming home, and sometimes he wrote letters to Nelly. The writing in them was uncertain, and the spelling was doubtful, but the love was safe enough. And when he had poured out his heart in small "i's" and capital "U's"? he always inquired how more material things were faring. "How's the herrings this sayson; and did the men do well with the mack'rel at Kinsale; and is the cowhouse new thatched, and how's the chapel going? And is the ould man still playing hang with the texes?"

Kinvig heard of Davy's prosperity, and received the news at first in silence, then with satisfaction, and at length with noisy pride. His boy was a bould fellow. "None o' yer randy-tandy-tissimee-tea tied to the old mawther's apron-strings about *him*. He's coming home rich, and he'll buy half the island over, and make a donation of a harmonia to the chapel, and kick ould Cowley and his fiddle out."

Awaiting that event, Kinvig sent Nelly to England, to be educated according to the station she was about to fill. Nelly was four years in Liverpool, but she had as many breaks for visits home. The first time she came she minced her words affectedly, and Kinvig whispered the mother that she was getting "a fine English tongue at her." The second time she came she plagued everybody out of peace by correcting their "plaze" to "please," and the "mate" to "meat," and the "lave" to "leave." The third time she came she was silent, and looked ashamed: and the fourth time it was to meet her sweetheart on his return home after ten years' absence.

Davy came by the Sneafell from Liverpool. It was August—the height of the visiting season—and the deck of the steamer was full of tourists. Davy walked through the cobweb of feet and outstretched legs with the face of a man who thought he ought to speak to everybody. Fifty times in the first three hours he went forward to peer through the wind and the glaring sunshine for the first glimpse of the Isle of Man. When at length he saw it, like a gray bird lying on the waters far away, with the sun's light tipping the hill-tops like a feathery crest, he felt so thick about the throat that he took six steerage passengers to the bar below to help him to get rid of his hoarseness. There was a brass band aboard, and during the trip they played all the outlandish airs of Germany, but just as the pacquet steamed into Douglas Bay, and Davy was watching the land and remembering everything upon it, and shouting "That's Castle Mona!" "There's Fort Ann!" "Yonder's ould St. Mathews's!" they struck up "Home, Sweet Home." That was too much for Davy. He dived into his breeches' pockets, gave every German of the troupe five shillings apiece, and then sat down on a coil of rope and blubbered aloud like a baby.

Kinvig had sent a grand landau from Ramsey to fetch Capt'n Davy to Ballaugh; but before the English driver from the Mitre had identified his fare Davy had recognized an old crony, with a high, springless, country cart—Billiam Ballaneddan, who had come to Douglas to dispatch a barrel of salted herrings to his married daughter at Liverpool, and was going back immediately. So Davy tumbled his boxes and bags and other belongings into the landau, piling them mountains high on the cushioned seats, and clambered into the cart himself. Then they set off at a race which should be home first—the cart or the carriage, the luggage or the owner of it; the English driver on his box seat with his tall hat and starchy cravat, or Billiam twidling his rope reins, and Davy on the plank seat beside him, bobbing and bumping, and rattling over the stones like a parched pea on a frying pan.

That was a tremendous drive for Davy. He shouted when he recognized anything, and as he recognized everything he shouted throughout the drive. They took the road by old Braddan Church and Union Mills, past St. John's, under the Tynwald Hill, and down Creg Willie's Hill. As he approached Kirk Michael his excitement was intense. He was nearing home and he began to know the people. "Lord save us, there's Tommy Bill-beg—how do, Tommy? And there's ould Betty! My gough, she's in yet—how do, mawther? There's little Juan Caine growed up to a man! How do, Johnny, and how's the girls and how's the ould man, and how's yourself? Goodness me, here's Liza Corlett, and a baby at her——! I knew her when she was no more than a babby herself." This last remark to the English driver who was coming up sedately with his landau at the tail of the springless cart.

"Drive on, Billiam! Come up, ould girl—just a taste of the whip, Billiam! Do her no harm at all. Bishop's Court! Deary me, the ould house is in the same place still."

At length the square tower of Ballaugh Church was seen above the trees with the last rays of the setting sun on its topmost story, and then Davy's eagerness swept down all his patience. He jumped up in the cart at the peril of being flung out, took off his billycock, whirled it round his head, bellowed "Hurrah! Hurrah! Hurrah!" After that he would have leaped alongside to the ground and run. "Hould hard!" he cried, "I'll bate the best mare that's going." But Billiam pinned him down to the seat with one hand while he whipped up the horse to a gallop with the other.

They arrived at Ballavolly an hour and a half before they were expected. Mistress Kinvig was washing dishes in a tub on the kitchen table. Kinvig himself was sitting lame with rheumatism in the "elber chair" by the ingle. They wiped down a chair for Davy this time.

"And Nelly," said Davy. "Where's Nelly?"

"She's coming, Capt'n," said Kinvig. "Nelly!" he called up the kitchen stairs, with a knowing wink at Davy, "Here's a gentleman asking after you."

Davy was dying of impatience. Would she be the same dear old Nell?

"Nell—Nelly," he shouted, "I've kep' my word."

"Aw, give her time, Capt'n," said Kinvig; "a new frock isn't rigged up in no time, not to spake of a silk handkercher going pinning round your throat."

But Davy, who had waited ten years, would not wait a minute longer, and he was making for the stairs with the purpose of invading Nell's own bedroom, when the lady herself came sweeping down on tiptoes. Davy saw her coming in a cloud of silk, and at the next moment the slippery stuff was crumbling, and whisking, and creaking under his hands, for his arms were full of it.

"Aw, mawther," said he. "They're like honeysuckles—don't spake to me for a week. Many's the time I've been lying in my bunk a-twigging the rats squeaking and coorting overhead, and thinking to myself, Kisses is skess with you now, Davy."

The wedding came off in a week. There were terrific rejoicings. The party returned from church in the landau that brought up Davy's luggage. At the bridge six strapping fellows, headed by the blacksmith, and surrounded by a troop of women and children, stretched a rope across the road, and would not let the horses pass until the bridegroom had paid the toll. Davy had prepared him-self in advance with two pounds in sixpenny bits, which made his trowsers pockets stand out like a couple of cannon balls. He fired those balls, and they broke in the air like shells.

At the wedding breakfast in the barn at Ballavolly Davy made a speech. It was a sermon to young fellows on the subject of sweethearts. "Don't you marry for land," said he. "It's muck," said he. "What d'ye say, Billiam—you'd like more of it? I wouldn't trust; but it's spaking the truth I am for all. Maybe you think about some dirty ould trouss: 'She's a warm girl, she's got nice things at her—bas'es and pigs, and the like of that.' But don't, if you'rr not a reg'lar blundering blockit." Then, looking down at the top of Nelly's head, where she sat with her eyes in her lap beside him, he softened down to sentiment, and said, "Marry for love, boys; stick to the girl that's good, and then go where you will she'll be the star above that you'll sail your barque by, and if you stay at home (and there's no place like it) her parting kiss at midnight will be helping you through your work all next day."

The parting kiss at midnight brought Davy's oration to a close, for a tug at his coat-tails on Nelly's side fetched him suddenly to his seat.

Two hours afterward the landau was rolling away toward the Castle Mona Hotel at Douglas, where, by Nell's arrangement, Capt'n Davy and his bride were to spend their honeymoon.

II

Now it so befell that on the very day when Capt'n Davy and Mrs. Quiggin quarreled and separated, two of their friends were by their urgent invitation crossing from England to visit them, Davy's friend was Jonathan Lovibond, an Englishman, whose acquaintance he had made on the coast. Mrs. Quiggin's was Jenny Crow, a young lady of lively manners, whom she had annexed during her four years' residence at Liverpool. These two had been lovers five years before, had quarreled and parted on the eve of the time appointed for their marriage, and had not since set eyes on each other. They met for the first time afterward on the steamer that was taking them to the Isle of Man, and neither knew the destination of the other.

Miss Crow looked out of her twinkling eyes and saw a gentleman promenading on the quarter-deck before her, whom she must have thought she had somewhere seen before, but that his gigantic black mustache was a puzzle, and the little imperial on his chin was a baffling difficulty. Mr. Lovibond puffed the smoke from a colossal cigar, and wondered if the world held two pair of eyes like those big black ones which glanced up at him sometimes from a deck stool, a puffy pile of wool, two long crochet needles, and a couple of white hands, from which there flashed a diamond ring he somehow thought he knew.

These mutual meditations lasted two long hours, and then a runaway ball of the wool from the lap of the lady on the deck stool was hotly pursued by the gentleman with the mustache, and instantly all uncertainty was at an end.

After exclamations of surprise at the strange recognition (it was all so sudden), the two old friends came to closer quarters. They touched gingerly on the past, had some tender passages of delicate fencing, gave various sly hits and digs, threw out certain subtle hints, and came to a mutual and satisfactory understanding. Neither had ever looked at anybody else since their rupture, and therefore both were still unmarried.

Having reached this stage of investigation, the wool and its needles were stowed away in a basket under the chair, in order that the lady might accept the invitation of the gentleman to walk with him on the deck; and as the wind had freshened by this time, and walking in skirts was like tacking in a stiff breeze, the gentleman offered his arm to the lady, and thus they sailed forth together.

"And with whom are you to stay when we reach the island, Jenny?" said Lovibond.

"With a young Manx friend lately married," said Jenny.

"That's strange; for I am going to do the same," said Lovibond. "Where?"

"At Castle Mona," said Jenny.

"That's stranger still; for it's the place to which I am going," said Lovibond. "What's your Manx friend's name?"

"Mrs. Quiggin, now," said Jenny.

"That's strangest of all," said Lovibond; "for my friend is Captain Quiggin, and we are bound for the same place, on the same errand."

This series of coincidences thawed down the remaining frost between the pair, and they exchanged mutual confidences. They had gone so far as to promise themselves a fortnight's further enjoyment of each other's society, when their arrival at Douglas put a sudden end to their anticipations.

Two carriages were waiting for them on the pier—one, with a maid inside, was to take Jenny to Castle Mona: the other, with a boy, was to take Lovibond to Fort Ann.

The maid was Peggy Quine, seventeen years of age, of dark complexion, nearly as round as a dolley-tub, and of deadly earnest temperament. When Jenny found herself face to face and alone with this person, she lost no time in asking how it came to pass that Mrs. Quiggin was at Castle Mona while her husband was at Fort Ann.

"They've parted, ma'am," said Peggy.

"Parted?" shrieked Jenny above the rattle of the carriage glass.

"Ah, yes, ma'am," Peggy stammered; "cruel, ma'am, right cruel, cruel extraordinary. It's a wonder the capt'n doesn't think shame of his conduck. The poor misthress! She's clane heartbroken. It's a mercy to me she didn't clout him."

In two minutes more Jenny was in Mrs. Quiggin's room at Castle Mona, crying, "Gracious me, Ellen, what is this your maid tells me?"

Nelly had been eating out her heart in silence all day long, and now the flood of her pride and wrath burst out, and she poured her wrongs upon Jenny as fiercely as if that lady stood for the transgressions of her husband.

"He reproached me with my poverty," she cried.

"What?"

"Well, he told me I had only married him for his money—there's not much difference."

"And what did you say?" said Jenny.

"Say? What could I say? What would any woman say who had any respect for herself?"

"But how did he come to accuse you of marrying him for his money? Had you asked him for any?"

"Not I, indeed."

"Perhaps you hadn't loved him enough?"

"Not that either—that I know of."

"Then why did he say it?"

"Just because I wanted him to respect himself, and have some respect for his wife, too, and behave as a gentleman, and not as a raw Manx rabbit from the Calf."

Jenny gave a look of amused intelligence, and said, "Oh, oh, I see, I see! Well, let me take off my bonnet, at all events."

While this was being done in the bedroom Nelly, who was furtively wiping her eyes, continued the recital of her wrongs:—

"Would you believe it, Jenny, the first thing he did when we arrived here after the wedding was to shake hands with the hall porter, and the boots who took our luggage, and ask after their sisters and their mothers, and their sweethearts—the man knew them all. And when he heard from his boy, Willie Quarrie, that the cook was a person from Michael, it was as much as I could do to keep him from tearing down to the kitchen to talk about old times."

"Yes, I see," said Jenny; "he has made a fortune, but he is just the same simple Manx lad that he was ten years ago."

"Just, just! We can't go out for a walk together but he shouts, 'How do? Fine day, mates!' to the drivers of the hackney cabs across the promenade; and the joy of his life is to get up at seven in the morning and go down to the quay before breakfast to keep tally with a chalk for the fishermen counting their herrings out of the boats into the barrels."

"Not a bit changed, then, since he went away?" said Jenny, before the glass.

"Not a bit; and because I asked him to know his place, and if he is a gentleman to behave as a gentleman and speak as a gentleman and not make so easy with such as don't respect him any the better for it, he turns on me and tells me I've only married him for his money."

"Dreadful!" said Jenny, fixing her fringe. "And is this the old sweetheart you have waited ten years for?"

"Indeed, it is."

"And now that he has come back and you've married him, he has parted from you in ten days?"

"Yes; and it will be the talk of the island—indeed it will."

"Shocking! And so he has left you here on your honeymoon without a penny to bless yourself?"

"Oh, for the matter of that, he fixed something on me before the wedding—a jointure, the advocates called it."

"Terrible! Let me see. He's the one who sent you presents from America?"

"Oh; he piled presents enough on me. It's the way of the men: the stingiest will do that. They like to think they're such generous creatures. But let a poor woman count on it, and she'll soon be wakened from her dream. 'You married me for my money—deny it?'"

"Fearful!"

Jenny was leaning her forehead against the window sash, and looking vacantly out on the bay. Nelly observed her a moment, stopped suddenly in the tale of her troubles, and said, in another voice, "Jenny Crow, I believe you are laughing at me. It's always the way with you. You can take nothing seriously."

Jenny turned back to the room with a solemn face, and said, "Nellie, if you waited ten years for your husband, I suppose that he waited ten years for you."

"I suppose he did."

"And, if he is the same man as he was when he went away, I suppose his love is the same?"

"Then how *could* he say such things?"

"And, if he is the same, and his love is the same, isn't it possible that somebody else is different?"

"Now, Jenny Crow, you are going to say it's all my fault?"

"Not all, Nelly. Something has come between you."

"It's the money. Oh, Jenny, if you ever marry, marry a poor man, and then he can't fling it in your face that you are poorer than he."

"No; it can't be the money, Nelly, for the money is his, and yet it hasn't changed him. And, Nelly, isn't it a good thing in a rich man not to turn his back on his old poor comrades—not to think because he has been in the sun that people are black who are only in the shade—not to pretend to have altered his skin because his coat has changed—isn't it?"

"I see what you mean. You mean that I've driven my husband away with my bad temper."

"No; not that; but Nelly—dear old Nell—think what you're doing. Take warning from one who once made shipwreck of her own life. Think no man common who loves you—no matter what his ways are, or his manners, or his speech. Love makes the true nobility. It ennobles him who loves you and you who are beloved. Cling to it—prize it—do not throw it away. Money can not buy it, nor fame nor rank atone for it. When a woman is loved she is a queen, and he who loves her is her king."

Mrs. Quiggin was weeping behind her hands by this time, but she lifted swollen eyes to say, "I see; you would have me go to him and submit, and explain, and beg his pardon. 'Dear David, I didn't marry you for your money——' No," leaping to her feet, "I'll scrub my fingers to the bone first."

"But, Nelly——"

"Say no more, Jenny Crow, We're hot-headed people, both of us, and we'll quarrel."

Then Jenny's solemn manner was gone in an instant. She snapped her fingers, kicked up one leg a little, and said lightly, "Very well; and now let us have some dinner,"——

Meantime Lovibond was hearing the other side of the story from Captain Davy at Forte Ann. On the way there he had heard of the separation from the boy, Willie Quarrie, a lugubrious Manx lad, eighteen years old, with a face as white as a haddock and as grim as a gannet.

"Aw, terr'ble doings, sir, terr'ble, terr'ble!" moaned Willie. "Young Mistress Quiggin ateing her heart out at Castle Mona, and Captain Davy hisself at Forte Ann over, drinking and tearing and carrying on till all's blue."

Lovibond found Captain Davy in the smoke-room with a face as hard as a frozen turnip, one leg over the arm of an elbow chair, a church-warden pipe in his mouth, a gigantic glass of brandy and soda before him, and an admiring circle of the laziest riff-raff of the town about him. As soon as they were alone he said:

"But what's this that your boy tells me, captain?"

"I'm foundered," said Davy, "broke, wrecked, the screw of my tide's gone twisting on the rocks. I'm done, mate, I'm done."

Then he proceeded to recite the incidents of the quarrel, coloring them by the light of the numerous glasses with which he had covered his brain since morning.

"'You've married me for my money,' says I. 'What else?' said she. 'Then d—— the money,' says I, 'I'll lave you till it's gone.' 'Do it and welcome,' says she, and I'm doing it, bad cess to it, I'm doing it. But, stop this jaw. I swore to myself I wouldn't spake of it to any man living. What d'ye drink? I've took to the brandy swig myself. Join in. Mate!" (this in a voice of thunder to the waiter at the end of the adjoining room) "brandy for the gentleman."

Lovibond waited a moment and then said quietly, "But whatever made you give her an ungenerous stab like that, captain?"

Davy looked up curiously and answered, "That's just what I've tooken six big drinks to find out. But no use at all, and what's left to do?"

"Why take it back?" said Lovibond.

"No, deng my buttons if I will."

"Why not?"

"'Cause it's true."

Lovibond waited again, and then said in another voice, "And is this the little girl you used to tell of out yonder on the coast—Nessy, Nelly, Nell, what was it?"

Davy's eyes began to fill, but his mouth remained firm. He cleared his throat noisily, shook the dust out of his pipe on to the heel of his boot, and said, "No—yes—no—Well, it is and it isn't. It's Nelly Kinvig, that's sarten sure. But the juice of the woman's sowl's dried up."

"The little thing that used to know your rap at the kitchen window, and come tripping out like a bird chirping in the night, and go linking down the lane with you in the starlight?"

Davy broke the shaft of his churchwarden into small lengths, and flung the pieces out at the open window and said, "I darn't say no."

"The one that stuck to you like wax when her father gave you the great bounce out—eh?"

Davy wriggled and spat, and then muttered, "You go bail."

"You have known her since you were children, haven't you?"

Davy's hard face thawed suddenly, and he said, "Ay, since she wore petticoats up to her knees, and I was a boy in a jacket, and we played hop-skotch in the haggard, and double-my-duck agen the cowhouse gable. Aw dear, aw dear! The sweet little thing she was then any way.

Yellow hair at her, and eyes like the sea, and a voice same as the throstle! Well, well, to think, to think! Playing in the gorse and the ling together, and the daisies and the buttercups—and then the curlews whistling and the river singing like music, and the bees ahumoning—aw, terr'ble sweet and nice. And me going barefoot, and her bare-legged, and divil a hat at the one of us—aw, deary me, deary me! Wasn't much starch at her in them ould days, mate."

"Is there now, captain?"

"Now? D'ye say *now*? My goodness! It's always hemming and humming and a heise of the neck, and her head up like a Cochin-China, with a topknot, and 'How d'ye do?' and cetererar and cetererar. Aw, smooth as an ould threepenny bit—smooth astonishing. And partic'lar! My gough! You couldn't call Tom to a cat afore her, but she'd be agate of you to make it Thomas."

Lovibond smiled behind his big mustache.

"The rael ould Manx isn't good enough for her now. Well, I wasn't objecting, not me. She's got the English tongue at her—that's all right. Only I'll stick to what I'm used of. Job's patience went at last and so did mine, and I arn't much of a Job neither."

"And what has made all this difference," said Lovibond.

"Why, the money, of coorse. It was the money that done it, bad sess to it," said Davy, pitching the head of his pipe after the shank. "I went out yonder to get it and I got it. Middling hard work, too, but no matter. It was to be all for her. 'I'll come back, Nelly,' says I, 'and we'll take Ballacry and have six craythurs and a pony, and keep a girl to do for you, and you'll take your aise—only milking maybe, or churning, but nothing to do no harm.' I was ten years getting it, and I never took notions on no other girls neither. No, honor bright, thinks I, Nelly's waiting for you, Davy. Always dreaming of her, 'cept when them lazy black chaps wanted leathering, and that's a job that isn't nothing without a bit of swearing at whiles. But at night, aw, at night, mate, lying out on the deck in that heat like the miller's kiln, and shelling your clothes piece by piece same as a bushel of oats, and looking up at the stars atwinkling in the sky, and spotting one of them, and saying to yourself quietlike, so as them niggers won't hear, 'That's star is atwinkling over Nelly, too, and maybe she's watching it now.' It seemed as if we wasn't so far apart then. Somehow it made the world a taste smaller. 'Shine on, my beauty,' thinks I, 'shine down straight into Nelly's room, and if she's awake tell her I'm coming, and if she's asleep just make her dream that I'm loving nobody else till her.' But, chut! It was myself that was dreaming. Drink up! She married me for my money, so I'm making it fly."

"And when it's gone—what then?" said Lovibond. "Will you go back to her!"

"Maybe so, maybe no."

"Will anything be the better because the money's spent?"

"God knows."

"Will she be as sweet and good as she once was when you are as poor as you were?"

Davy heaved up to his feet. "What's the use of thinking of the like of that?" he cried. "My money's mine, I baked for it out in that oven. Now I'm spending it, and what for shouldn't I? Here goes—healths apiece!"

Next day Lovibond and Jenny Crow met on the pier. There they pondered the ticklish situation of their friends, and every word they said on it was pointed and punctuated by a sense of their own relations.

"It's plain that the good fools love each other," said Jenny.

"Quite plain," said Lovibond.

"Heigho! It's mad work being angry with somebody you are dying to love," said Jenny.

"Colney Hatch is nothing to it," said Lovibond.

"Smaller things have parted people for years," said Jenny.

"Yes; five years," said Lovibond.

"The longer apart the wider the breach, and the harder to cover it," said Jenny.

"Just so," said Lovibond.

"They must meet. Of course they'll fight like cat and dog, but better that than this separation. Time leaves bigger scars than claws ever made. Now, couldn't we bring them together?"

"Just what I was thinking," said Lovibond.

"I'm sure he must be a dear, simple soul, though I've never set eyes on him," said Jenny.

"And I'm certain she must be as sweet as an angel, though I've never seen her," said Lovibond.

Jenny shot a jealous glance at her companion, then cracked two fingers and said eagerly, "There you are—there's the idea in a cockle-shell. Now *if each could see the other through other eyes!*"

"The very thing!" said Lovibond.

"Then why don't you give me your arm at once, and let me think me over?" said Jenny. In less than an hour these two wise heads had devised a scheme to bring Capt'n Davy and his bride together. What that scheme was and how it worked let those who read discover.

III

Six days passed as with feet of lead, and Capt'n Davy and Mrs. Quiggin were still in Douglas. They could not tear themselves away. Morning and night the good souls were seized by a morbid curiosity about their servants' sweethearts. "Seen Peggy lately?" Capt'n Davy would say. "I suppose you've not come across Willie Quarrie lately?" Mrs. Quiggin would ask. Thus did they squeeze to the driest pulp every opportunity of hearing anything of each other.

Jenny Crow, with Mrs. Quiggin at Castle Mona, had not yet set eyes on Captain Davy, and Lovibond, with Captain Davy at Fort Ann, had never once seen Mrs. Quiggin. Jenny had said nothing of Lovibond to Nelly, and Lovibond had said nothing of Jenny to Davy.

Matters stood so when one evening Peggy Quine was dressing up her mistress's hair for dinner, and answering the usual question.

"Seen Willie Quarrie, ma'am? Aw 'deed, yes, ma'am; and it's shocking the stories he's telling me. The Capt'n's making the money fly. Bowls and beer, and cards and betting—it's ter'ble, ma'm, ter'ble. Somebody should hould him. He's distracted like. Giving to everybody as free as free. Parsons and preachers and the like—they're all at him, same as flies at a sheep with the rot."

"And what do people say, Peggy?"

"They say fools and their money is quickly parted ma'am."

"How dare you call anybody a fool, Peggy?"

"Aw it's not me, ma'am. It's them that's seeing him wasting his money like water through a pitchfork. And the dirts that's catching most is shouting loudest. 'Deed, ma'am, but his conduct is shocking."

"And what do people say is the cause of it, Peggy?"

"Lumps in his porridge, ma'am."

"What?"

"Yes, though, that's what Willie Quarrie is telling me. When a woman isn't just running even with her husband they call her lumps in his porridge. Aw, Willie's a feeling lad."

There was a pause after this disclosure, and then Mrs. Quiggin said in another voice, "Peggy, there's a strange gentleman staying with the Captain at Forte Ann, is there not?"

"Yes, ma'am; Mr. Loviboy."

"What is he like, Peggy?"

"Pepper and salt trowis, ma'am, and a morsel of hair on the tip of his chin."

"Tall, Peggy?"

"No, a long wisp'ry man."

"I suppose he helps the Captain to spend his money?"

"Never a ha'po'th, ma'am, 'deed no; but ter'ble onaisy at it, and rigging him constant But no use at all, at all. The Capt'n's intarmined to ruin hisself. Somebody should just take him and wallop him, ding dong, afore he's wasted all he's got, and hasn't a penny left at him."

"How dare you, Peggy?"

Peggy was dismissed in anger, and Mrs. Quiggin sat down to write a letter to Lovibond. She begged him to pardon the liberty of one who was no stranger, though they had never met, in asking him to come to her without delay. This done, and marked *private*, she called Peggy back and bade her to take the letter to Willie Quarrie, and tell him to give it to the gentleman before the Captain came down to breakfast in the morning.

The day was Sunday, the weather was brilliant, the window was open, and the salt breath of the sea was floating into the room. With the rustle of silk like a breeze in a pine tree Jenny Crow came back from a walk, swinging a parasol by a ring about her wrist.

"Such an adventure!" she said, sinking into a chair. "A man, of course! I saw him first on the Head at the skirts of the crowd that was listening to the Bishop's preaching. Such a manly fellow! Broad-shouldered, big-chested, standing square on his legs like a rock. Dark, of course, and such eyes, Nelly! Brown—no black-brown. I like black-brown eyes in a man, don't you?"

Captain Davy's eyes were of the darkest brown. Mrs. Quiggin gave no sign.

"Then his dress—so simple. None of your cuffs and ruffs, and great high collars like a cart going for coke. Just a blue serge suit, and a monkey jacket. I like a man in a monkey jacket."

Captain Davy wore a monkey jacket; Mrs. Quiggin colored slightly.

"A sailor, thinks I. There's something so free and open about a sailor, isn't there?"

"Do you think so, Jenny?" said Mrs. Quiggin in a faint voice.

"I'm sure of it, Nelly. The sailor is just like the sea. He's noisy—so is the sea. Liable to storms—so is the sea. Blusters and boils, and rocks and reels—so does the sea. But he's sunny too, and open and free, and healthy and bracing, and the sea is all that as well."

Mrs. Quiggin was thinking of Captain Davy, and tingling with pleasure and shame, but she only said, falteringly, "Didn't you talk of some adventure?"

"Oh, of course, certainly," said Jenny. "After he had listened a moment he went on, and I lost sight of him. Presently I went on, too, and walked across the Head until I came within sight of Port Soderick. Then I sat down by a great bowlder. So quiet up there, Nelly; not a sound except the squeal of the sea birds, the boo-oo of the big waves outside, and the plash-ash of the little ones on the beach below. All at once I heard a sigh. At that I looked to the other side of the bowlder, and there was my friend of the monkey jacket. I was going to rise, but he rose instead, and begged me not to trouble. Then I was vexed with myself, and said I hoped he wouldn't disturb himself on my account."

"You never said that, Jenny Crow?"

"Why not, my dear? You wouldn't have had me less courteous than he was. So he stood and talked. You never heard such a voice, Nelly. Deep as a bell, and his Manx tongue was like music. Talk of the Irish brogue! There's no brogue in the world like the Manx, is there now, not if the right man is speaking it."

"So he was a Manxman," said Mrs. Quiggin, with a far-away look through the open window.

"Didn't I say so before? But he has quite saddened me. I'm sure there's trouble hanging over him. 'I've been sailing foreign, ma'am,' said he, 'and I don't know nothing—'."

"Oh, then he wasn't a gentleman?" said Mrs. Quiggin.

Jenny fired up sharply. "Depends on what you call a gentleman, my dear. Now, any man is a gentleman to me who can afford to dispense with the first two syllables of the name."

Mrs. Quiggin looked down at her feet.

"I only meant," she said meekly, "that your friend hasn't as much education—."

"Then, perhaps, he has more brains," said Jenny. "That's the way they're sometimes divided, you know, and education isn't everything."

"Do *you* think that, Jenny?" said Mrs. Quiggin, with another long look through the window.

"Of course I do," said Jenny.

"And what did he say?"

"'I've been sailing foreign, ma'am,' he said. 'And I don't know nothing that cut's a man's heart from its moorings like coming home same as a homing pigeon, and then wishing yourself back again same as a lost one.'"

"Poor fellow!" said Mrs. Quiggin. "He must have found things changed since he went away."

"He must," said Jenny.

"Perhaps he has lost some one who was dear to him," said Mrs. Quiggin.

"Perhaps," said Jenny, with a sigh.

"His mother may be, or his sister—" began Mrs. Quiggin.

"Yes, or his wife." continued Jenny, with a moan.

Mrs. Quiggin drew up suddenly. "What's his name?" she asked sharply.

"Nay, how could I ask him that?" said Jenny.

"Where does he live?" said Mrs. Quiggin.

"Or that either?" said Jenny.

Mrs. Quiggin's eyes wandered slowly back to the window. "We've all got our troubles, Jenny," she said quietly.

"All," said Jenny. "I wonder if I shall ever see him again."

"Tell me if you do, Jenny?" said Mrs. Quiggin.

"I will, Nelly," said Jenny.

"Poor fellow, poor fellow," said Mrs. Quiggin.

As Jenny rose to remove her bonnet she shot a sly glance out of the corners of her eyes, and saw that Mrs. Quiggin was furtively wiping her own.

Meanwhile Lovibond at Fort Ann was telling a similar story to Captain Davy. He had left the house for a walk before Davy had come down to breakfast, and on returning at noon he found him immersed in the usual occupation of his mornings. This was that of reading and replying to his correspondence. Davy read with difficulty, and replied to all letters by check. His method of business was peculiar and original. He was stretched on the sofa with a pipe in his mouth, and the morning's letters pigeonholed between his legs. Willie Quarrie sat at a table with a check-book before him. While Davy read the letters one by one he instructed Willie as to the nature of the answer, and Willie, with his head aslant, his mouth awry, and his tongue in his cheek, turned it into figures on the check-book.

As Lovibond came in Davy was knocking off the last batch for the day. "'Respected sir,' he was reading, 'I know you've a tender heart'. . . Send her five pounds, Willie, and tell her to take that talk to the butchers."

"'Honored Captain, we are going to erect a new school in connection with Ballajora chapel, and if you will honor us by laying the foundation stone. . .' Never laid a stone in my life 'cept one, and that was my mawther's sink-stone. Twenty pounds, Willie. 'Sir, we are to hold a bazaar, and if you will consent to open it. . .' Bazaar! I know: a sort of ould clothes shop in a chapel where you're never tooken up for cheating, because you always says your paternoster-ings afore you begin. Ten pounds, Willie. Helloa, here's Parson Quiggin. Wish the ould devil would write more simpler; I was never no good at the big spells myself. 'Dear David. . .' That's good—he walloped me out of the school once for mimicking his walk—same as a coakatoo esactly. 'Dear David, owing to the lamentable death of brother Mylechreest it has been resolved to ask you to become a member of our committee. . .' Com-mittee! I know the sort—kind of religious firm where there's three partners, only two of them's sleeping ones. Dirty ould hypocrite! Fifteen pounds, Willie."

This was the scene that Lovibond interrupted by his entrance. "Still bent on spending your money, Captain?" he said. "Don't you see that the people who write you these begging letters are impostors?"

"Coorse I do," said Davy. "What's it saying in the Ould Book? 'Where the carcass is, there will the eagles be gathered together.' Only, as Parson Howard used to say, bless the ould angel, 'Summat's gone screw with the translation theer, friends, should have been vultures.'"

"Half of them will only drink your money, Captain," said Lovibond.

"And what for shouldn't they? That's what I'm doing," said Davy.

"It's poor work, Captain, poor work. You didn't always think: money was a thing to pitch into a ditch."

"Always? My goodness, no!" said Davy. "Time was once when I thought money was just all and Tommy in this world. My gough, yes, when I was a slip of a lad, didn't I?" said he, sobering very suddenly. "The father was lost in a gale at the herrings, and the mawther had to fend for the lot of us. They all went off except myself—the sisters and brothers. Poor things, they wasn't willing to stay with us, and no wonder. But there's mostly an ould person about every Manx house that sees the young ones out, and the mawther's father was at us still. Lame though of his legs with the rheumatics, and wake in his intellecs for all. Couldn't do nothing but lie in by the fire with his bit of a blanket hanging over his head, same as snow atop of a hawthorn bush. Just stirring the peats, and boiling the kettle, and lifting the gorse when there was any fire. The mawther weeded for Jarvis Kewley—sixpence a day dry days, and fourpence all weathers. Middling hard do's, mate. And when she'd give the ould man his basin of broth he'd be saying, squeaky-like, 'Give it to the boy, woman; he's a growing lad?' 'Chut! take it, man,' the mawther would say, and then he'd be whimpering, 'I'm keeping you long, Liza, I'm keeping you long.' And there was herself making a noise with her spoon in the bottom of a basin, and there was me grinding my teeth, and swearing to myself like mad, 'As sure as the living God I'll be ruch some day.' And now—"

Davy snapped his fingers, laughed boisterously, rolled to his feet, and said shortly, "Where've you been to?"

"To church—the church with a spire at the end of the parade," said Lovibond.

"St. Thomas's—I know it," said Davy.

St. Thomas's was half way up to Castle Mona.

The men strolled out at the window, which opened on to the warm, soft turf of the Head, and lay down there with their faces to the sun-lit bay.

"Who preached?" said Davy, clasping hands at the back of his head.

"A young woman," said Lovibond.

Davy lifted his head out of its socket, "My goodness!" he said.

"Well, at all events," explained Lovibond, "it was a girl who preached to *me*. The moment I went into the church I saw her, and I saw nothing else until I came out again."

Davy laughed, "Ay, that's the way a girl slips in," said he. "Who was she?"

"Nay; I don't know," said Lovibond; "but she sat over against me on the opposite side of the aisle, and her face was the only prayer-book I could keep my eyes from wandering from."

"And what was her tex', mate?"

"Beauty, grace, truth, the tenderness of a true heart, the sweetness of a soul that is fresh and pure."

Davy looked up with vast solemnity. "Take care," said he. "There's odds of women, sir. They're like sheep's broth is women. If there's a heart and head in them they're good, and if there isn't you might as well be supping hot water. Faces isn't the chronometer to steer your boat to the good ones. Now I've seen some you could swear to——."

"I'll swear to this one," said Lovibond with an appearance of tremendous earnestness.

Davy looked at him, gravely. "D'ye say so?" said he.

"Such eyes, Capt'n—big and full, and blue, and then pale, pale blue, in the whites of them too, like—like——."

"*I* know," said Davy; "like a blackbird's eggs with the young birds just breaking out of them."

"Just," said Lovibond, "And then her hair, Capt'n—brown, that brown with a golden bloom, as if it must have been yellow when she was a child."

"I know the sort, sir," said Davy, proudly; "like the ling on the mountains in May, with the gorse creeping under it."

"Exactly. And then her voice, Captain, her voice—."

"So you were speaking to her?" said Davy.

"No, but didn't she sing?" said Lovibond. "Such tones, soft and tremulous, rising and falling, the same as—as—."

"Same as the lark's, mate," said Davy, eagerly; "same as the lark's—first a burst and a mount and then a trimble and a tumble, as if she'd got a drink of water out of the clouds of heaven, and was singing and swallowing together—I know the sort; go on."

Lovibond had kept pace with Davy's warmth, but now he paused and said quietly, "I'm afraid she's in trouble."

"Poor thing!" said Davy. "How's that, mate?"

"People can never disguise their feelings in singing a hymn," said Lovibond.

"You say true, mate," said Davy; "nor in giving one out neither. Now, there was old Kinvig. He had a sow once that wasn't too reg'lar in her pigging. Sometimes she gave many, and sometimes she gave few, and sometimes she gave none. She was a hit-and-a-missy sort of a sow, you might say. But you always know'd how the ould sow done, by the way Kinvig gave out the hymn. If it was six he was as loud as a clarnet, and if it was one his voice was like the tram-bones. But go on about the girl."

"That's all," said Lovibond. "When the service was over I walked down the aisle behind her, and touched her dress with my hand, and somehow—."

"I know," cried Davy. "Gave you a kind of 'lectricity shock, didn't it? Lord alive, mate, girls is quare things."

"Then she walked off the other way," said Lovibond.

"So you don't know where she comes from?" said Davy.

"I couldn't bring myself to follow her, Capt'n."

"And right too, mate. It's sneaking. Following a girl in the streets is sneaking, and the man that done it ought to be wallopped till all's blue.

HALL CAINE

But you'll see her again, I'll go bail, and maybe hear who she is. Rael true women is skess these days, sir; but I'm thinking you've got your flotes down for a good one. Give her line, mate—give her line—and if I wasn't such a downhearted chap myself I'd be helping you to land her."

Lovibond observed that Capt'n Davy was more than usually restless after this conversation, and in the course of the afternoon, while he lay in a hazy dose on the sofa, he overheard this passage between the captain and his boy:—

"Willie Quarrie, didn't you say there was an English lady staying with Mistress Quiggin at Castle Mona?"

"Miss Crows; yes," said Willie. "So Peggy Quine is telling me—a little person with a spyglass, and that fond of the mistress you wouldn't think."

"Then just slip across in the morning, and spake to herself, and say can I see her somewheres, or will she come here, and never say nothing to nobody."

Davy's uneasiness continued far into the evening. He walked alone to and fro on the turf of the Head in front of the house, until the sun set behind the hills to the west, where a golden rim from its falling light died off on the farthest line of the sea to the east, and the town between lay in a haze of deepening purple. Lovibond knew where his thoughts were, and what new turn they had taken; but he pretended to see nothing, and he gave no sign.

Sunday as it was, Capt'n Davy's cronies came as usual at nightfall. They were a sorry gang, but Davy welcomed them with noisy cheer. The lights were brought in, and the company sat down to its accustomed amusements. These were drinking and smoking, with gambling in disguise at intervals. Davy lost tremendously, and laughed with a sort of wild joy at every failure. He was cheated on all hands, and he knew it. Now and again he called the cheaters by hard name, but he always paid them their money. They forgave the one for the sake of the other, and went on without shame. Lovibond's gorge rose at the spectacle. He was an old gambler himself, and could have stripped every rascal of them all as naked as a lettuce after a locust. His indignation got the better of him at last, and he went out on to the Head.

The calm sea lay like a dark pavement dotted with the reflection of the stars overhead. Lights in a wide half-circle showed the line of the bay. Below was the black rock of the island of the Tower of Refuge, and the narrow strip of the old Red pier; beyond was the dark outline of the

Head, and from the seaward breast of it shot the light of the lighthouse, like the glow of a kiln. It was as quiet and beautiful out there as it had been noisy and hideous within.

Lovibond had been walking to and fro for more than an hour listening to the slumberous voices of the night, and hearing at intervals the louder bellowing from the room where Captain Davy and his cronies were sitting, when Davy himself came out.

"I can't stand no more of it, and I've sent them home," he said. "It's like saying your prayers to a hornpipe, thinking of her and carrying on with them wastrels."

He was sober in one sense only.

"Tell me more about the little girl in church. Aw, matey, matey! Something under my waistcoat went creep, creep, creep, same as a sarpent, when you first spake of her; but its easier to stand till that jaw inside anyway. Go on, sir. Love at first sight, was it? Aw, well, the eyes isn't the only place that love is coming in at, or blind men would all be bachelors. Now mine came in at the ear."

"Did you fall in love with her singing, Capt'n?" said Lovibond.

"Yes, did I," said Davy, "and her spaking, too, and her whispering as well, but it wasn't music that brought love in at my ear—my left ear it was, Matey."

"Whatever was it then, Capt'n," said Lovibond.

"Milk," said Davy.

"Milk?" cried Lovibond, drawing up in their walk.

"Just milk," said Davy again. "Come along and I tell you. It was this way. Ould Kinvig kep' two cows, and we were calling the one Whitie and the other Brownie. Nelly and me was milking the pair of them, and she was like a young goat, that full of tricks, and I was same as a big calf, that shy. One evening—it was just between the lights—that's when girls is like kittens, terr'ble full of capers and mischievousness—Nelly rigged up her kopie—that's her milking-stool—agen mine, so that we sat back to back, her milking Brownie and me milking Whitie. 'What she agate of now?' thinks I, but she was looking as innocent as the bas'es themselves, with their ould solem faces when they were twisting round. Then we started, and there wasn't no noise in the cow-house, but just the cows chewing constant, and, maybe, the rope running on their necks at whiles and the rattle of the milk in the pails. And I got to draeming same as I was used of, with the smell of the hay stealing down from the loft and the breath of the cows coming puff when they were blowing, and the tits in my hands agoing, when the rattle-rattle aback of me stopped sudden, and I felt a squish in my ear like the syringe at the doctor's. 'What's that?' thinks I. 'Is it deaf I'm going?' But it's deaf I'd been and blind, too, and stupid for all down to that blessed minute, for there was Nessy laughing like fits, and working like mad, and drops of Brownie's milk going trickling out of my ear on to my shoulder. 'It's not deafness,' thinks I; 'it's love'; and my breath was coming and going and making noises like the smithy bellows. So I twisted my wrist and blazed back at her, and we both fired away, ding-dong, till the cows was as dry as Kinvig when he was teetotal, and the cow-house was like a snowstorm with a gale of wind through it, and you couldn't see a face at the one of us for swansdown. That's how Nelly and me 'came engage."

He was laughing noisily by this time, and crying alternately, with a merry shout and a husky croak, "Aw, dear, aw, dear; the days that was, sir—the days that was!"

Lovibond let him rattle on, and he talked of Nelly for an hour. He had stories without end of her, some of them as simple as a baby's prattle, some as deep as the heart of man, and splitting open the very crust of the fires of buried passion.

It was late when they turned in for the night. The lights on the line of the land were all put out, and save for the reflection of the stars only the lamps of ships at anchor lit up the waters of the bay.

"Good night, capt'n," said Lovibond. "I suppose you'll go to bed now?"

"Maybe so, maybe no," said Davy. "You see, I'm like Kinvig these days, and go to bed to do my thinking. The ould man's cart-wheel came off in the road once, and we couldn't rig it on again no how. 'Hould hard, boys,' says Kinvig; and he went away home and up to the loft, and whipped off his clothes, and into the blankets and stayed there till he'd got the lay of that cartwheel. Aw, yes, though—thinking, thinking, thinking constant—that's me when I'm in bed. But it isn't the lying awake I'm minding. Och, no; it's the wakening up again. That's like nothing in the world but a rusty nail going driving into your skull afore a blacksmith's seven-pound sledge. Good night, mate; good night."

IV

Next day Lovibond saw Mrs. Quiggin at Castle Mona. He had come at once in obedience to her summons, and she took his sympathies by storm. It was hard for him to realize that he had not seen her somewhere before. He *had* seen her—in his own description of the girl in church, helped out, led on, directed, vivified, and transfigured by Capt'n Davy's own impetuous picture, just as the mesmerist sees what he pretends to show by aid of the eye of the mesmerized. There she sat, like one for whom life had lost its savor. Her great slow eyes, her pale and quivering face,' her long deep look as she took his hand, and her softly tightening grasp of it went through him like a knife. Not all his loyalty to Capt'n Davy could crush the thought that the man who had thrown away a jewel such as this must be a brute and a blockhead. But the sweet woman was not so lost to life that she did not see her advantage. There were some weary sighs and then she said:—

"I am in great, great trouble about my husband. They say he is wasting his money. Is it true?"

"Too true," said Lovibond.

"And that if he goes on as he is now going he will be penniless?"

"Not impossible," said Lovibond, "provided the mad fit last long enough."

"Is remonstrance quite useless, Mr. Lovibond?"

"Quite, Mrs. Quiggin."

The great slow eyes began to fill, and Lovibond's gaze to seek the laces of his boots.

"It is sorrow enough to me, Mr. Lovibond, that my husband and I have quarreled and parted, but it will be the worst grief of all if some day I should have to think that I came into his life to wreck it."

"Don't blame yourself for that, Mrs. Quiggin. It will be his own fault if he ruins himself."

"You are very good, Mr. Lovibond."

"Your husband will never blame you either."

"That will hardly reconcile me to his misfortunes."

["The man's an ass," thought Lovibond.]

"I shall not trouble him much longer with my presence here," Mrs. Quiggin continued, and Lovibond looked up inquiringly.

"I am going back home soon," she added. "But if before I go some friend would help me to save my husband from himself——"

Lovibond rose in an instant. "I am at your service, Mrs. Quiggin," he said briskly. "Have you thought of anything?"

"Yes. They tell me that he is gambling, and that all the cheats of the island are winning from him."

"Well?"

The pale face turned very red, and quivered visibly about the lips.

"I have heard him say, when he has spoken of you, Mr. Lovibond, that—that—but will you forgive what I am going to tell you?"

"Anything," said Lovibond.

"That out on the coast *you* could win from anybody. I remembered this when they told me that he was gambling, and I thought if you would play against my husband—for *me*——"

"I see what you mean, Mrs. Quiggin," said Lovibond.

"I don't want the money, though he was so cruel as to say I had only married him for sake of it. But you could put it back into Dumbell's Bank day by day as you got it."

"In whose name?" said Lovibond.

The great eyes opened very wide. "His, surely," she said falteringly.

Lovibond saw the folly of that thought, but he also recognized its tenderness.

"Very well," he said; "I'll do my best."

"Will it be wrong to deceive him, Mr. Lovibond?"

"It will be mercy itself, Mrs. Quiggin."

"To be sure, it is only to save him from ruin. But you will not believe that I am thinking of myself, Mr. Lovibond?"

"Trust me for that, Mrs. Quiggin."

"And when the wild fit is over, and my husband hears of what has been done, you will be careful not to let him know that it was I who thought of it?"

"You shall tell him yourself, Mrs. Quiggin."

"Ah! that can never, never be," she said, with a sigh. And then she murmured softly, "I don't know what my husband may have told you about me, Mr. Lovibond—."

Lovibond's ardor overcame his prudence. "He has told me that you were an angel once—and he has wronged you, the dunce and dulbert— you are an angel still."

While Lovibond was with Mrs. Quig-gin Jenny Crow was with Capt'n Davy. She had clutched at his invitation with secret delight. "Just the thing," she thought. "Now, won't I give the other simpleton a piece of my mind, too?" So she had bowled off to Fort Ann with a heart as warm as toast, and a tongue that was stinging hot. But when she had got there her purpose had suddenly changed. The first sight of Capt'n Davy's face had conquered her. It was so child-like, and yet so manly, so strong and yet so tender, so obviously made for smiles like sunshine, and yet so full of the memories of recent tears! Jenny recalled her description of the sailor on the Head, and thought it no better than a vulgar caricature.

Davy wiped down a chair for her with the outside of his billycock and led her up to it with rude but natural manners. "The girl was a ninny to quarrel with a man like this," she thought. Nevertheless she remembered her purpose of making him smart, and she stuck to her guns for a round or two.

"It's rael nice of you to come, ma'am," said Davy.

"It's more than you deserve," said Jenny.

"I shouldn't wonder but you think me a blundering blocket," said Davy.

"I didn't think you had sense enough to know it," said Jenny.

With that second shot Jenny's powder was spent. Davy looked down into her face and said—

"I'm terr'ble onaisy about herself, ma'am, and can't take rest at nights for thinking what's to come to her when I am gone."

"Gone?" said Jenny, rising quietly.

"That's so ma'am," said Davy. "I'm going away—back to that ould Nick's oven I came from, and I'll want no money there."

"Is that why you're wasting it here, Captain Quiggin?" said Jenny. Her gayety was gone by this time.

"No—yes! Wasting? Well maybe so, ma'am, may be so. It's the way with money. Comes like the droppings out of the spout at the gable, ma'am; but goes like the tub when the bull has tipped it. Now I was thinking ma'am——"

"Well, Captain?"

"She won't take any of it, coming from me, but I was thinking, ma'am—"

"Yes?" Davy was pawing the carpet with one foot, and Jenny's eyes were creeping up the horn buttons of his waistcoat.

"I was thinking, ma'am, if you could take a mossle of it yourself

HALL CAINE

before it's all gone, and go and live with her—you and she together somewheres—some quiet place—and make out somehow—women's mortal clever at rigging up yarns that do no harm—make out that somebody belonging to you is dead—it can't kill nobody to say that ma'am—and left you a bit of a fortune out of hand——"

Davy's restless foot was digging away at the carpet while he was stammering out these broken words:

"Haven't you no ould uncle, ma'am, that would do for the like of that?"

Jenny had to struggle with herself not to leap up and hug Capt'n Davy then and there, "What a ninny the girl was!" she thought. But she said aloud, as well as she could for her throat that was choking her, "I see what you mean, Captain Quiggin. But, Captain——"

"Ma'am?" said Davy.

"If you have so much thought—(*gulp, gulp*)—for your wife's welfare (*gulp*), you—must love her still (*gulp, gulp*)?"

"I daren't say no, ma'am," said Davy, with downcast eyes.

"And if you love her, however deeply she may have offended you, surely you should never leave her. Come, now, Captain, forgive and forget; she is only a woman, you know."

"That's just where the shoe pinches, ma'am, so I'm taking it off. Out yonder it'll be easier to forgive. And if it'll be harder to forget, what matter?"

Jenny's eyes were beginning to fill.

"No use crying over spilled milk, is it, ma'am? The heart-ache is a sort of colic that isn't cured by drops."

Jenny was breaking down fast.

"Aw, the heart's a quare thing, ma'am. Got its hunger same as anything else. Starve it, and it'll know why. Gives you a kind of a sinking at the pit of your stomach, ma'am. Did you never feel it, ma'am?"

Davy's speech was rude enough, but that only made its emotion the more touching to Jenny. Between gulp and gulp she tried to say that if he went away he would never be happy again.

"Happy, ma'am? D'ye say happy? I'm not happy *now*," said Davy.

"It isn't everybody would think so, Captain," said Jenny, "considering how you spend your evenings—singing and laughing——"

"Laughing! More cry till wool, ma'am, same as clipping a pig."

"So your new friends, Captain, those that your riches have brought you—"

"Friends? D'ye say friends? Them wastrels! What are they? Nothing but a parcel of Betty Quilleash's baby's stepmothers. And I'm nothing but Betty Quilleash's baby myself, ma'am; that's what I am."

The stalwart fellow did not look much like anybody's infant, but Davy could not laugh, and Jenny's eyes were streaming.

"Betty lived at Michael, ma'am, and died when her baby was suckling. There wasn't no feeding-bottles in them days, and the little one was missing the poor dead mawther mortal. But babies is like lammies, ma'am, they've got their season, and mostly all the women of the parish had babies that year. So first one woman would whip up Betty's baby and give it a taste of the breast, and then another would whip it up and do likewise, until the little baby cuckoo was in every baby nest in the place, and living all over the street, like the rum-butter bowl and the preserving pan. But no use at all, at all. The little mite wasted away. Poor thing, poor thing. Twenty mawthers wasn't making up to it for the right one it had lost. That's me, ma'am; that's me."

Jenny Crow went away, crying openly, having promised to be a party to the innocent deception which Captain Davy had suggested. "That Nelly Kinvig is as hard as a flint," she told herself, bitterly. "I've no patience with such flinty people; and won't I give it her piping hot at the very next opportunity?"

V

J enny's opportunity was a week in coming, and various events of some consequence in this history occurred in the mean time. The first of these was that Capt'n Davy's fortune changed hands.

Davy's savings had been invested in two securities—the Liverpool Dock Trust and Dumbell's Manx Bank. His property in the former he made over by help of the advocates, and with vast show of secrecy, to the name of Jenny Crow; and she, on her part, by help of other advocates, and with yet more real secrecy, transferred it to the name of Mrs. Quiggin.

The remains of his possessions in the latter he lost to Lovibond, who gambled with him constantly, beginning with a sovereign, which Mrs. Quiggin had lent him for the purpose, and going on by a process of doubling until the stakes were prodigious. Every night he discharged his debt by check on Dumbell's, and every morning Lovibond repaid it into the same bank to the account of his wife. Thus, within a week, unknown to either of the two persons chiefly concerned, the money which had been the immediate cause of strife between them passed from the offender to the offended, from the strong to the weak.

That was the more material of the changes that had come to pass, and the more spiritual were of still greater consequence.

Lovibond and Jenny met constantly. They made various excursions through the island—to the Tynwald Hill, to Peel Castle, to Castle Rushen, the Chasms, and the Calf. Of course they persuaded each other that these trips were taken solely in the interests of their friends. It was necessary to meet; it was desirable to do so where they would be unobserved; what else was left to them but to steal away together on these little jaunts and journeys?

Then their talk was of love and estrangement and reconciliation, and how easy to quarrel, and how hard to come together again. Capt'n Davy and Mrs. Quiggin provided all their illustrations to these interesting themes, for naturally they never spoke of themselves.

"It's astonishing what geese some people can be," said Jenny.

"Astonishing," echoed Lovibond.

"Just for sake of a poor little word of confession to hold off like this," said Jenny.

"Just a poor little word," said Lovibond.

"He has only to say 'My dear, I behaved like a brute,' but——"

"Only that," said Lovibond. "And she has merely to say, 'My love, I behaved like a cat,' but——"

"That's all," said Jenny. "But he doesn't—men never do."

"Never," said Lovibond. "And she won't—women never will."

Then there would be innocent glances on both sides, and sly hints cast out as grappling hooks for jealousy.

"Ah, well, he's the dearest, simplest, manliest fellow in the world, and there are women who would give their two ears for him," said Jenny.

"And she's the sweetest, tenderest, loveliest woman alive, and there are men who would give their two eyes for her," said Lovibond.

"Pity they don't," said Jenny, "for all the use they make of them."

Amid such bouts of thrust and counter-thrust, the affair of Capt'n Davy and Mrs. Quiggin nevertheless made due progress.

"She's half in love with my Manx sailor on the Head," said Jenny.

"And he's more than half in love with my lady in the church," said Lovibond.

"And now that we've made each of them fond of each other in disguise, we have just to make both of them ashamed of themselves in reality," said Jenny.

"Just that," said Lovibond.

"Ah me," said Jenny. "It isn't every pair of geese that have friends like us to prevent them from going astray."

"It isn't," said Lovibond. "We're the good old ganders that keep the geese together."

"Speak for yourself, sir," said Jenny.

Then came Jenny's opportunity. She had been out on one of her jaunts with Lovibond, leaving Mrs. Quiggin alone in her room at Castle Mona. Mrs. Quiggin was still in her room, and still alone. Since the separation a fortnight before that had been the constant condition of her existence. Never going out, never even going down for her meals, rarely speaking of her husband, always thinking of him, and eating out her heart with pride and vexation, and anger and self-reproach.

It was the hour when the life of the island rises to the fever point; the hour of the arrival of the steamers from England. All day long the town had droned and dosed under a drowsy heat. The boatmen and carmen, with both hands in their breeches' pocket, had been burning the daylight on the esplanade; the band on the pier had been blowing music out of lungs that snored between every other blast; and the visitors had been lolling on the seats of the parade and watching the sea gulls disporting on the bay with eyes that were drawing straws. But the first trail of smoke had been seen across the sea by the point of the lighthouse, and all the slugs and marmots were wide awake: promenade deserted, streets quiet and pothouses empty; but every front window of every front house occupied, and the pier crowded with people looking seaward. "She's the Snaefell?" "No, but the Ben-my-Chree—see, she has four funnels." Then, the steaming up, the firing of the gun, the landing of the passengers, the mails and newspapers, the shouting of the touts, the bawling of the porters, the salutations, the welcomes, the passings of the time of day, the rattling of the oars, the tinkling of the trams, and the cries of the newsboys: "This way for Castle Mona!" "Falcon Cliff this way!" "Echo!" "Evening Express!" "Good passage, John?" "Good." "Five hours?" "And ten minutes." "What news over the water?" "They've caught him." "Never." "Express!" "Fort Anne here— here for Villiers." "Comfortable lodgings, sir." "Take a card, ma'am." "What verdict d'ye say?" "She's got ten years." "Had fine weather in the island?" "Fine." "Echo! Evening Echo!" "Fort Anne this way!" "Gladstone in Liverpool?" "Yes, spoke at Hengler's last night—fearful crush." "Castle Mona!" "Evening News!" "Peveril!" "This way Falcon Cliff!" "Ex-press!"

Thus, leaving the pier and the steamers behind them, through the streets and into the hotels, the houses, the cars, and the trains go, the new comers, and the newspapers, and the letters from England, all hot and active, bringing word of the main land, with its hub-bub and hurly-burly, to the island that has been four-and-twenty hours cut off from it—like the throbbing and bounding globules of fresh blood fetching life from the fountain-head to some half-severed limb. It is an hour of tremendous vitality, coming once a day, when the little island pulsates like a living thing. But that evening, as always since the time of the separation, Mrs. Quiggin was unmoved by it. With a book in her hand she was sitting by the open window fingering the pages, but looking listlessly over the tops of them to the line of the sea and sky, and asking herself if she should not go home to her father's house on the morrow. She had reached that point of her reverie at which something told her that she should, and something else told her that she should not, when down came Jenny Crow upon her troubled quiet, like the rush of an evening breeze.

"Such news!" cried Jenny. "I've seen him again."

Mrs. Quiggin's book dropped suddenly to her lap. "Seen him?" she said with bated breath.

"You remember—the Manx sailor on the Head," said Jenny.

"Oh!" said Mrs. Quiggin, languidly, and her book went back to before her face.

"Been to Laxey to look at the big wheel," said Jenny; "and found the Manxman coming back in the same coach. We were the only passengers, and so I heard everything. Didn't I tell you that he must be in trouble?"

"And is he?" said Mrs. Quiggin, monotonously.

"My dear," said Jenny, "he's married."

"I'm very sorry," said Mrs. Quiggin, with a listless look toward the sea. "I mean," she added more briskly, "that I thought you liked him yourself."

"Liked him!" cried Jenny. "I loved him. He's splendid, he's glorious, he's the simplest, manliest, tenderest, most natural creature in the world. But it's just my luck—another woman has got him. And such a woman, too! A nagger, a shrew, a cat, a piece of human flint, a thankless wretch, whose whole selfish body isn't worth the tip of his little finger."

"Is she so bad as that?" said Mrs. Quiggin, smiling feebly above the top edge of her book, which covered her face up to the mouth.

"My dear," said Jenny, solemnly, "she has turned him out of the house."

"Good gracious!" said Mrs. Quiggin; and away went the book on to the sofa.

Then Jenny told a woeful tale, her eyes flashing, her lips quivering, and her voice ringing with indignation. And, anxious to hit hard, she hovered so closely over the truth as sometimes to run the risk of uncovering it. The poor fellow had made long voyages abroad and saved some money. He had loved his wife passionately—that was the only blot on his character. He always dreamt of coming home, and settling down in comfort for the rest of his life. He had come at last, and a fine welcome had awaited him. His wife was as proud as Lucifer—the daughter of some green-grocer, of course. She had been ashamed of her husband, apparently, and settling down hadn't suited her. So she had nagged the poor fellow out of all peace of mind and body, taken his money, and turned him adrift.

Jenny's audacity carried her through, and Mrs. Quiggin, who was now wide awake, listened eagerly. "Can it be possible that there are women like that?" she said, in a hushed whisper.

"Indeed, yes," said Jenny; "and men are simple enough to prefer them to better people."

"But, Jenny," said Mrs. Quiggin, with a far-away look, "we have only heard one story, you know. If we were inside the Manxman's house—if we knew all—might we not find that there are two sides to its troubles?"

"There are two sides to its street-door," said Jenny, "and the husband is on the outside of it."

"She took his money, you say, Jenny?"

"Indeed she did, Nelly, and is living on it now."

"And then turned him out of doors?"

"Well, so to speak, she made it impossible for him to live with her."

"What a cat she must be!" said Mrs. Quiggin.

"She must," said Jenny. "And, would you believe it, though she has treated him so shamefully yet he loves her still."

"Why do you think so, Jenny," said Mrs. Quiggin.

"Because," said Jenny, "though he is always sober when I see him I suspect that he is drinking himself to death. He said as much."

"Poor fellow!" said Mrs. Quiggin. "But men should not take these things so much to heart. Such women are not worth it."

"No, are they?" said Jenny.

"They have hardly a right to live," said Mrs. Quiggin.

"No, have they?" said Jenny.

"There should be a law to put down nagging wives the same as biting dogs," said Mrs. Quiggin.

"Yes, shouldn't there?" said Jenny.

"Once on a time men took their wives like their horses on trial for a year and a day, and really with some women there would be something to say for the old custom."

"Yes, wouldn't there?" said Jenny.

"The woman who is nothing of herself apart from her husband, and has no claim to his consideration, except on the score of his love, and yet uses him only to abuse him, and takes his very 'money, having none of her own, and still——"

"Did I say she took his money, Nelly?" said Jenny. "Well of course—not to be unfair—some men are such generous fools, you know—he may have given it to her."

"No matter; taken or given, she has got it, I suppose, and is living on it now."

"Oh, yes, certainly, that's very sure," said Jenny; "but then she's his wife, you see, and naturally her maintenance——"

"Maintenance!" cried Mrs. Quig-gin. "How many children has she got?"

"None," said Jenny. "At least I haven't heard of any."

"Then she ought to be ashamed of herself for thinking of such a thing."

"I quite agree with you, Nelly," said Jenny.

"If I were a man," said Mrs. Quiggin, "and my wife turned me out of doors——"

"Did I say that, Nelly? Well not exactly that—no, not turned him out of doors exactly, Nelly."

"It's all one, Jenny. If a woman behaves so that her husband can not live with her what is she doing but turning him out of doors?"

"But, Nelly!" cried Jenny, rising suddenly. "What about Captain Davy?"

Then there was a blank silence. Mrs. Quiggin had been borne along on the torrent of her indignation, brooking no objection, and sweeping down every obstacle, until brought up sharply by Jenny's question—like a river that flows fastest and makes most noise where the bowlders in its course are biggest, but breaks itself at last against the brant sides of some impassable rock. She drew her breath in one silent spasm, turned from feverish red to deadly pale, quivered about the mouth, twitched about the eyelids, rose stiffly on her half-rigid limbs, and then fell on Jenny with loud and hot reproaches.

"How dare you, Jenny Crow?" she cried.

"Dare what, my dear?" said Jenny.

"Say that I've turned my husband out of doors, and that I've taken his money, and that I am a cat and shrew, and a nagger, and that there ought to be a law to put me down."

"My dear Nelly," said Jenny, "it was yourself that said so. I was speaking of the wife of the Manx sailor."

"Yes, but you were thinking of me," said Mrs. Quiggin.

"I was thinking of her," said Jenny.

"You were thinking of me as well," said Mrs. Quiggin.

"I tell you that I was only thinking of her," said Jenny.

"You were thinking of me, Jenny Crow—you know you were; and you meant that I was as bad as she was. But circumstances alter cases, and my case is different. My husband is turning *me* out of doors: and, as for his money, I didn't ask for it and I don't want it. I'll go back home to-morrow morning. I will—indeed, I will. I'll bear this torment no longer."

So saying, with many gasps and gulps, breaking at last into a burst of weeping, she covered her face with both hands and flounced out of the room. Jenny watched her go, then listened to the sobs that came from the other side of the door, and said beneath her breath, "Let her cry, poor girl. The crying has to be done by somebody, and it might as well be she. Crying is good for a woman sometimes, but when a man cries it hurts so much."

Half an hour later, as Jenny was leaving the room for dinner, she heard Mrs. Quiggin telling Peggy Quine to ask at the office for her bill, and to order a carriage to be ready at the door for her at eleven o'clock in the morning.

When the first burst of her vexation was spent Mrs. Quiggin made a secret and startling discovery. The man whom Jenny Crow had stumbled upon, first on the Head and afterward on the Laxey coach, could be no one in the world but her own husband. A certain shadowy suspicion of this had floated hazily before her mind at the beginning, but she had dismissed the idea and forgotten it. Now she felt so sure of it that it was beyond contempt of question. So the Manx sailor in whom Jenny had found so much to admire—the simple, brave, manly, generous, natural soul, all fresh air and by rights all sunshine—was no other than Capt'n Davy Quiggin! That thought brought the hot blood tingling to Mrs. Quiggin's cheeks with sensations of exquisite delight, and never before had her husband seemed so fine in her own eyes as now, when she saw him so noble in the eyes of another. But close behind this delicious reflection, like the green blight at the back of the apple blossom, lay a withering and cankering thought. The Manx sailor's wife—she who had so behaved that it was impossible for him to live with her—she who was a cat, a shrew, a nagger, a thankless wretch, a piece of human flint, a creature that should be put down by the law as it puts down biting dogs—she whose whole selfish body was not worth the tip of his little finger—was no one else than herself!

Then came another burst of weeping, but this time the tears were of shame, not of vexation, and they washed away every remaining evil humor and left the vision clear. She had been in the wrong, she was judged out of her own mouth; but she had no intention of fitting on the cap of the unknown woman. Why should she? Jenny did not know who the woman was—that was as plain as a pickle. Then where was the good of confessing?

VI

While Jenny Crow was doing her easy duty at Castle Mona, Lovibond was engaged in a task of yet more simplicity at Fort Ann. On returning from Laxey he found Captain Davey occupied with Willie Quarrie in preparations for a farewell supper to be given that night to the cronies who had helped him to spend his fortune. These worthies had deserted his company since Lovibond had begun to take all the winnings, including some of their own earlier ones; and hence the necessity to invite them. "There's ould Billy, the carrier—ask him," Davy was saying, as he lay stretched on the sofa, puffing whorls of gray smoke from a pipe of thick twist. "And then there's Kerruish, the churchwarden, and Kewley, the crier, and Hugh Corlett, the blacksmith, and Tommy Tubman, the brewer, and Willie Qualtrough, that keeps the lodging-house contagious, and the fat man that bosses the Sick and Indignant society, and the long, lanky shanks that is the headpiece of the Friendly and Malevolent Association—got them all down, boy?"

"They're all through there in my head already, Capt'n," groaned Willie Quarrie in despair, as he struggled at the table to keep pace with his slow pen to Davy's impetuous tongue.

"Then ask whosomever you plaze, boy," said Davy. "What's it saying in the ould Book: 'Go out into the highways and hedges and compel them to come in.' Only it's the back-courts and the public-houses this time, and you'll be wanting no grappling hooks to fetch them. Just whip a whisky bottle under your arm, and they'll be asking for no other invitation. Reminds me, sir," he added, looking up as Lovibond entered, "reminds me of little Jimmy Quayle's aisy way of fetching poor Hughie Collister from the bottom of Ramsey harbor. Himself and Hughie were same as brothers—that thick—and they'd been middling hard on the drink together, and one night Hughie, going home to Andreas, tumbled over the bridge by the sandy road and got hisself washed away and drowned. So the boys fetched grapplings and went out immadient to drag for the body, but Jimmy took another notion. He rigged up a tremenjous long pole, like your mawther's clothes' prop on washing day and tied a string to the top of it, and baited the end of the string with an empty bottle of Ould Tom, and then sat hisself down on the end of the jetty, same as a man that's going fishing. 'Lord-a-massy, Jemmy,' says the boys, looking up out of the boat; 'whatever in the name of goodness are you doing there?' 'They're telling me,' says Jemmy, bobbing the gin-bottle up and down constant, flip-a-flop, flip-a-flop atop of the water; 'they're telling me,' says he, 'that poor ould Hughie is down yonder, and I'm thinking there isn't nothing in the island that'll fetch him up quicker till this.'"

"But what is going on here, Capt'n?" said Lovibond, with an inclination of his head toward the table where Willie Quarrie was still laboring with his invitations.

"It's railly wuss till ever, sir," groaned Willie from behind his pen.

"What does it mean?" said Lovibond.

"It manes that I'm sailing to-morrow," said Davy.

"Sailing!" cried Lovibond.

"That's so," said Davy. "Back to the ould oven we came from. Pacific steamer laves Liverpool by the afternoon tide, and we'll catch her aisy if we take the 'Snaefell' in the morning. Fixed a couple of berths by telegraph, and paid through Dumbell's. Only ninety pounds the two—for'ard passage—but nearly claned out at that. What's the odds though? Enough left to give the boys a blow-out to-night, and then, heigho! stone broke, cut your stick and get out of it."

"A couple of berths? Did you say two?" said Lovibond.

"I'm taking Willie along with me," said Davy; "and he's that joyful at the thought of it that you can't get a word out of him for hallelujahs."

Willie's joy expressed itself at that moment in a moan, as he rose from the table with a woe-begone countenance, and went out on his errand of invitation.

"But you'll stay on," said Davy, "Eh?"

"No," said Lovibond, in a melancholy voice.

"Why not, then?" said Davy.

Lovibond did not answer at once, and Davy heaved up to a sitting posture that he might look into his face.

"Why, man; what's this—what's this?" said Davy. "You're looking as down as ould Kinvig at the camp meeting, when the preacher afore him had used up all his tex'es. What's going doing?"

Lovibond settled himself on the sofa beside Davy, and drew a deep breath. "I've seen her again, Capt'n," he said, solemnly.

"The sweet little lily in the church, sir?" said Davy.

"Yes," said Lovibond; and, after another deep breath, "I've spoken to her."

"Out with it, sir; out with it," said Davy, and then, putting one hand on Lovibond's knee caressingly, "I've seen trouble in my time, mate; you may trust me—go on, what is it?"

"She's married," said Lovibond.

Davy gave a prolonged whistle. "That's bad," he said. "I'm symperthizing with you. You've been fishing with another man's floats and losing your labor. I'm feeling for you. 'Deed I am."

"It's not myself I'm thinking of," said Lovibond. "It's that angel of a woman. She's not only married, but married to a brute."

"That's wuss still," said Davy.

"And not only married to a brute," said Lovibond, "but parted from him."

Davy gave a yet longer whistle. "O-ho, O-ho! A quarrel is it?" he cried. "Husband and wife, eh? Aw, take care, sir, take care. Women is 'cute. Extraordinary wayses they've at them of touching a man up under the watch-pocket of the weskit till you'd never think nothing but they're angels fresh down from heaven, and you could work at the docks to keep them; but maybe cunning as ould Harry all the time, and playing the divil with some poor man. It's me for knowing them. Husband and wife? That'll do, that'll do. Lave them alone, mate, lave them alone."

"Ah, the sweet creature has had a terrible time of it!" said Lovibond, lying back and looking up at the ceiling.

"I lave it with you," said Davy, charging his pipe afresh as a signal of his neutrality.

"He must have led her a fearful life," continued Lovibond.

Davy lit up, and puffed vigorously.

"It would appear," said Lovibond, "that though she is so like a lady, she is entirely dependent upon her husband."

"Well, well," said Davy, between puff and puff.

"He didn't forget that either, for he seems to have taunted her with her poverty."

A growl, like an oath half smothered by smoke, came from Davy.

"Indeed, that was the cause of quarrel."

"She did well to lave him," said Davy, watching the coils of his smoke going upward.

"Nay, it was he who left her."

"The villain!" said Davy. But after Davy had delivered himself so there was nothing to be heard for the next ten seconds but the sucking of lips over the pipe.

"And now," said Lovibond, "she can not stir out of doors but she finds herself the gossip of the island, and the gaze of every passer-by."

"Poor thing, poor thing!" said Davy.

HALL CAINE

"He must be a low, vulgar fellow," said Lovibond; "and yet—would you believe it?—she wouldn't hear a word against him."

"The sweet woman!" said Davy.

"It's my firm belief that she loves the fellow still," said Lovibond.

"I wouldn't trust," said Davy. "That's the ways of women, sir; I've seen it myself. Aw, women is quare, sir, wonderful quare."

"And yet," said Lovibond, "while she is sitting pining to death indoors he is enjoying himself night and day with his coarse companions."

Davy put up his pipe on the mantelpiece. "Now the man that does the like of that is a scoundrel," he said, warmly.

"I agree with you, Capt'n," said Lovibond.

"He's a brute!" said Davy, more loudly.

"Of course we've only heard one side of the story," said Lovibond.

"No matter; he's a brute and a scoundrel," said Davy. "Dont you hould with me there, mate?"

"I do," said Lovibond. "But still—who knows? She may—I say she may—be one of those women who want their own way."

"All women wants it," said Davy. "It's mawther's milk to them— Mawther Eve's milk, as you might say."

"True, true!" said Lovibond; "but though she looks so sweet she may have a temper."

"And what for shouldn't she?" said Davy, "D'ye think God A'mighty meant it all for the men?"

"Perhaps," said Lovibond, "she turned up her nose at his coarse ways and rough comrades."

"And right, too," said Davy. "Let him keep his dirty trousses to hisself. Who is he?"

"She didn't tell me that," said Lovibond.

"Whoever he is he's a wastrel," said Davy.

"I'm afraid you're right, Capt'n," said Lovibond.

"Women is priv'leged where money goes," said Davy. "If they haven't got it by heirship they can't make it by industry, and to accuse them of being without it is taking a mane advantage. It's hitting below the belt, sir. Accuse a man if you like—ten to one he's lazy—but a woman— never, sir, never, never!"

Davy was tramping the room by this time, and making it ring with the voice as of a lion, and the foot as of an elephant.

"More till that, sir," he said. "A good girl with nothing at her who takes a bad man with a million cries talley with the crayther the day she marries him. What has he brought her? His dirty, mucky, measley money, come from the Lord knows where. What has *she* brought him? Herself, and everything she is and will be, stand or fall, sink or swim, blow high, blow low—to sail by his side till they cast anchor together at last Don't you hould with me there, sir?"

"I do, Capt'n, I do," said Lovibond.

"And the ruch man that goes bearing up alongside a girl that's sweet and honest, and then twitting her with being poorer till hisself, is a dirt and divil, and ought to be walloped out of the company of dacent men."

"But, Capt'n," said Lovibond, falteringly! "Capt'n. . . ."

"What?"

"Wasn't Mrs. Quiggin a poor girl when you married her?"

At that word Davy looked like a man newly awakened from a trance. His voice, which had rung out like a horn, seemed to wheeze back like a whistle; his eyes, which had begun to blaze, took a fixed and stupid look; his lips parted; his head dropped forward; his chest fell inward; and his big shoulders seemed to shrink. He looked about him vacantly, put one hand up to his forehead and said in a broken underbreath, "Lord-a-massy! What am I doing? What am I saying?"

The painful moment was broken by the arrival of the first of the guests. It was Keruish, the churchwarden, a very-secular person, deep in the dumps over a horse which he had bought at Castletown fair the week before (with money cheated out of Davy), and lost by an attack of the worms that morning. "Butts in the stomach, sir," he moaned; "they're bad, sir, aw, they're bad."

"Nothing wuss," said Davy. "I know them. Ate all the goodness out of you and lave you without bowels. Men has them as well as horses—only we call (them) friends instead."

The other guests arrived one by one—the blacksmith, the crier, the brewer, the lodging-house keeper, and the two secretaries of the charitable societies (whose names were "spells" too big for Davy), and the keeper of a home for lost dogs.

They were a various and motley company of the riff-raff and raggabash of the island,—young and elderly, silent and glib—rough as a pigskin, and smooth as their sleeves at the elbow; with just one feature common to the whole pack of pick-thanks, and that was a look of shallow cunning.

Davy received them with noisy welcomes and equal cheer, but he had the measure of every man of them all, down to the bottom of their fob pockets. The cloth was laid, the supper was served, and down they sat at the table.

"Anywhere, anywhere!" cried Davy, as they took their places. "The mate is the same at every seat."

"Ay, ay," they laughed, and then fell to without ceremony.

"Only wait till I've done the carving, and we'll all start fair," said Davy.

"Coorse, coorse," they answered, from mouths half full already.

"That's what Kinvig said when he was cutting up his sermon into firstly, secondly, thirdly, and fourteenthly."

"Ha, ha! Kinvig! I'd drink the ould man's health if I had anything," cried the blacksmith, with a wink at his opposite neighbor.

"No liquor?" said Davy, looking up to sharpen the carving knife on the steel. "Am I laving you dry like herrings in the hould?"

"Season us, capt'n," cried the black-smith, amid general laughter from the rest.

"Aw, lave you alone for that," said Davy. "If you're like myself you're in pickle enough already."

Then there were more winks and louder laughter.

"Mate!" shouted Davy over his shoulder to the waiter behind him, "a gallon to every gentleman."

"Ay, ay," from all sides of the table in various tones of satisfaction.

"Yes, sir—of course, sir; beg pardon, sir, here, sir," said the waiter.

"Boys, healths apiece!" cried Davy.

"Healths apiece, Capt'n!" answered numerous thick voices, and up leaped a line of yellow glasses.

"Ate, drink—there's plenty, boys; there's plenty," said Davy.

"Aw, plenty, capt'n—plenty."

"Come again, boys, come again," said Davy, from time to time; "but clane plates—aw, clane plates—I hould with being nice at your males for all, and no pigging."

Thus the supper went on for an hour, and then Davy by way of grace said, "Praise the Lord, O my soul, and all that is within me, praise His holy name."

"A 'propriate tex', too," said the church-warden. "Aw, it's wonderful the scriptural the Captn's getting when he's a bit crooked," he whispered behind the back of his hand.

After that Davy stretched back in his chair and cried, "Your pipes in your faces, boys. Smook up, smook up; chimleys everywhere, same as Douglas at breakfast time."

For Davy's sake Lovibond had sat at table with the guests, though their voracity had almost turned his stomach. At sight of the green light of greed in their eyes he had said to himself, "Davy is a rough fellow, but a born Christian. These creatures are hogs. Why doesn't his gorge rise at them?" When the supper was done, and while the cloth was being removed, amid the clatter of dishes and the striking of lights, Lovibond rose and slipped out of the room.

Davy saw him go, and from that moment he became constrained and silent. Sucking at his pipe and devoting himself steadily to the drink, he answered in *hum's and ha's and that'll do's* to the questions put to him, and his laughter came out of him at intervals in jumps and jerks like water from the neck of a bottle.

"What's agate of the Capt'n?" the men whispered. "He's quiet to-night—quiet uncommon."

After a while Davy heaved up and followed Lovibond. He found him walking too and fro in the soft turf outside the window. The night was calm and beautiful. In the sky a sea of stars and a great full moon; on the land a line of gas jets, and on the dark bay a point here and there of rolling light. No sound but the distant hum of traffic in the town, the inarticulate shout of a sailor on one of the ships outside, and the rock-row rock-row of the oars in the rol-locks of some unseen boat gliding into the harbor below.

Davy drew a long breath. "So you think," said he, "that the sweet woman in the church is loving her husband in spite of all?"

"Fear she is, poor fool," said Lovibond.

"Bless her!" said Davy, beneath his breath. "D'ye think, now," said he, "that all women are like that?"

"Many are—too many," said Lovibond.

"Equal to forgiving and forgetting, eh?" said Davy.

"Yes—the sweet simpletons—and taking the men back as well," said Lovibond.

"Extraordinary!" said Davy. "Aw, matey, matey, men's only muck where women comes. Women is reg'lar eight-teen-carat goold. It's me to know it too. There was the mawther herself now. My father was a bit of a rip—God forgive his son for saying it—and once he went trapsing after a girl and got her into trouble. An imperent young hussy anyway, but no matter. Coorse the mawther wouldn't have no truck with her; but one day she died sudden, and then the child hadn't nobody but the neighbors to look to it. 'Go for it, Davy,' says the mawther to me. It was evening, middling late after the herrings, and when I got to the kitchen windey there was the little one atop of the bed in her nightdress saying her bits of prayers; 'God bless mawther, and everybody,' and all to that. She couldn't get out of the 'mawther' yet, being always used of it, and there never was no 'father' in her little tex'es. Poor thing! she come along with me, bless you, like a lammie that you'd pick out of the snow. Just hitched her hands round my neck and fell asleep in my arms going back, with her putty face looking up at the stars same as an angel's— soft and woolly to your lips like milk straight from the cow, and her little body smelling sweet and damp, same as the breath of a calf. And when the mawther saw me she smoothed her brat and dried her hands, and catched at the little one, and chuckled over her, and clucked at her and kissed her, with her own face slushed like rain, till yer'd have thought nothing but it was one of her own that had been lost and was found agen. Aw, women for your life, mate, for forgiveness.'"

Lovibond did not speak, and Davy began to laugh in a husky voice.

"Bless me, the talk a man will put out when he's a bit over the rope and thinking of ould times," he said.

"Sign that I'm thirsty," he added; and then walked toward the window. "But the father could never forgive hisself," he said, as he was stepping through, "and if I done wrong to a woman neither could I—I've that much of the ould man in me anyway."

When he got back to the room the air was dense with tobacco-smoke, and his guests were shouting for his company. "Capt'n Davy!" "Where's Capt'n Davy?" "Aw, here's the man himself?" "Been studying the stars, Capt'n?" "Well, that's a bit of navigation." "Navigation by starlight—I know the sort. Navigating up alongside a pretty girl, eh, Capt'n?"

There were rough jokes, and strange stories, and more liquor and loud laughter, and for a time Davy took his part in everything. But after a while he grew quiet again, and absent in manner, and he glanced up at intervals in the direction of the window, A new thought had come to him. It made the sweat to break out at the top of his forehead, and then he heard no more of the clatter around him than the rum-humdrum as of a train in a tunnel, pierced sometimes by the shrill scream as of an occasional whistle. Presently he rolled up again, and went out once more to Lovibond.

The thought that had seized him was agony, and he could not broach it at once. So he beat about it for a moment, and then came down on it with a crash.

"Sitting alone, is she, poor thing?" he said.

"Alone," said Lovibond.

"I know, I know," said Davy. "Like a bird on a bough calling mournful for her mate; but he's gone, he's down, maybe worse, but lost anyway. Yet if he should ever come back now—eh?"

"He'll have to be quick then," said Lovibond; "for she intends to go home to her people soon."

"Did you say she was for going home?" said Davy, eagerly. "Home where—where to—to England?"

"No," said Lovibond. "Havn't I told you she's a Manx woman?"

"A Manx woman, is she?" said Davy. "What's her name?"

"I didn't ask her that," said Lovibond.

"Then where's her home?" said Davy.

"I forget the name of the place," said Lovibond. "Balla—something."

"Is it—— is it——" Davy was speaking very quickly—"is it Ballaugh, sir?"

"That's it," and Lovibond. "And her father's farm—I heard the name of the farm as well—Balla—balla—something else—oh, Ballavalley."

"Ballavolly?" said Davy.

"Exactly," said Lovibond.

Davy breathed heavily, swayed slightly, and rolled against Lovibond as they walked side by side.

"Then you know the place, Capt'n," said Lovibond.

Davy laughed noisily. "Ay, I know it," he said.

"And the girl's father, too, I suppose?" said Lovibond.

Davy laughed bitterly. "Ay, and the girl's father too," he said.

"And the girl herself perhaps?" said Lovibond.

Davy laughed almost fiercely, "Ay, and the girl herself," he said.

Lovibond did not spare him. "Then," said he, in an innocent way, "you must know her husband also."

Davy laughed wildly. "I wouldn't trust," he said.

"He's a brute—isn't he?" said Lovibond.

"Ugh!" Davy's laughter stopped very suddenly.

"A fool, too—is he not?" said Lovibond.

"Ay—a damned fool!" said Davy out of the depths of his throat, and then he laughed and reeled again, and gripped at Lovibond's sleeve to keep himself erect.

"Helloa!" he cried, in another voice; "I'm rocking full like a ship with a rolling cargo and my head is as thick as Taubman's brewery on boiling day."

He was a changed man from that instant onward. An angel of God that had been breathing on his soul was driven out by a devil of despair. The conviction had settled on him that he was a dastard. Lovibond remembered the story of his father? and trembled for what he had done.

Davy stumbled back through the window into the room, singing lustily—

> O, Molla Char—aine, where got you your gold?
> Lone, lone, you have le—eft me here,
> O, not in the Curragh, deep under the mo—old,
> Lone, lo—one, and void of cheer,
> Lone, lo—one, and void of cheer.

His cronies received him with shouts of welcome. "You'll be walking the crank yet, Capt'n," said they, in mockery of his unsteady gait. His altered humor suited them. "Cards," they cried; "cards—a game for good luck."

"Hould hard," said Davy. "Fair do's. Send for the landlord first."

"What for?" they asked. "To stop us? He'll do that quick enough."

"You'll see," said Davy. "Willie," he shouted, "bring up the skipper."

Willie Quarrie went out on his errand, and Davy called for a song. The Crier gave one line three times, and broke down as often. "I linger round this very spot—I linger round this ve—ery spot—I linger round this very—"

"Don't do it any longer, mate," cried Davy. "Your song is like Kinvig's first sermon. The ould man couldn't get no farther till his tex', so he gave it out three times—'I am the Light of the World—I am the Light of the World—I am the Light—' 'Maybe so, brother,' says ould Kennish, in the pew below; 'but you want snuffing. Come down out of that.'"

Loud peals of wild laughter followed, and Davy's own laughter rang out wildest and maddest of all. Then up came the landlord with his round face smiling. What was the Captain's pleasure?

"Landlord," cried Davy, "tell your men to fill up these glasses, and then send me your bill for all I owe you, and make it cover everything I'll want till to-morrow morning."

"To-morrow will do for the bill, Captain," said the landlord. "I'm not afraid that you'll cut your country."

"Aren't you, though? Then the more fool you," said Davy. "Send it up, my shining sunflower; send it up."

"Very well, Captain, just to humor you," said the landlord, backing himself out with his head in his chest.

"Why, where are you going to, Capt'n?" cried many voices at once.

"Wherever there's a big cabbage growing, boys," said Davy.

The bill came up, and Willie Quarrie examined it. "Shocking!" cried Willie; "it's really shocking! Shillings apiece for my breakfas'es—now that's what I call a reg'lar piece of ambition."

Davy turned out his pockets on to the table. The pockets were many, and were hidden away, back and front and side, in every slack and tight place in his clothes. Gold, silver, and copper came mixed and loose from all of them, and he piled up the money in a little heap before him. When all was out he picked five sovereigns from the haggis of coin and put them back into his waistcoat pocket, while he screwed up one eye into the semblance of a wink, and said to Willie, "That'll see us over." Then he called for a sight of the bill, glanced at the total and proceeded to count out the amount of it. This being done, he rolled the money in the paper, screwed it up like a penny worth of lozenges, and sent it down to the landlord with his bes' respec's. After that he straightened his chest, stuck his thumbs in the arm-holes of his waistcoat, nodded his head downward at the money remaining on the table and said, "Men, see that? It's every ha'penny I'm worth in the world, A month ago I came home with a nice warm fortune at me. That's what's left, and when it's gone I'm up the spout."

The men looked at each other in blank surprise, and began to mutter among themselves, "What game is he agate of now?" "Aw, it's true." "True enough, you go bail." "I wouldn't trust, he's been so reckless." "Twenty thousands, they're saying." "Aw, he's been helped—there's that Mister Loviboy, a power of money the craythur must have had out of him." "Well, sarve him right; fools and their money is rightly parted."

Thus they croaked and crowed, and though Davy was devoting himself to the drink he heard them.

A wild light shot into his eyes, but he only laughed more noisily and talked more incessantly.

"Come, lay down, d'ye hear," he cried. "Do you think I care for the fortune? I care nothing, not I. I've had a bigger loss till that in my time."

"Lord save us, Capt'n—when?" cried one.

"Never mind when—not long ago, any way," said Davy.

"And you had heart to start afresh, Cap'n, eh?" cried another.

"Heart, you say? Maybe so, maybe no," said Davy. "But stow this jaw.

Here's my harvest home, boys, my Melliah, only I am bringing back the tares—who's game to toss for it? Equal stakes, sudden death!"

The brewer tossed with him and won. Davy brushed the money across the table, and laughed more madly than ever. "I care nothing, not I, say what you like," he cried again and again, though no one disputed his protestation.

But the manner of the cronies changed toward him nevertheless. Some fell to patronizing him, some to advising him, and some to sneering at the hubbub he was making.

"Well, well," he cried, "One glass and a toast, anyway, and part friends for all." "Aisy there! silence! Hush? Chink up! (Hear, hear?) Are you ready? Here goes, boys? The biggest blockit in the island, bar none—Capt'n Davy Quiggin."

At that the raggabash who had been clinking glasses pretended to be mightily offended in their dignity. They looked about for their hats, and began to shuffle out.

"Lave me, then; lave me," cried Davy. "Lave me, now, you Noah's ark of creeping things. Lave me, I'm stone broke. Ay, lave me, you dogs with your noses in the snow. I'm done, I'm done."

As the rascals who had cheated and robbed him trooped out like men aggrieved, Davy broke out into a stave of another wild song:

"I'm hunting the wren," said Bobbin to Bobbin,
"I'm hunting the wren," said Richard to Robbin,
"I'm hunting the wren," said Jack of the Lhen,
"I'm hunting the wren," said every one.

When the men were gone Lovibond came back by the window. The room was dense with the fumes of dead smoke, and foul with the smell of stale liquor. Broken pipes lay on the table amid the refuse of spilled beer, and a candle, at which the pipes had been lighted, still stood there burning.

Davy was reeling about madly, and singing and laughing in gust on gust. His face was afire with the drink that he had taken, and his throat was guggling and sputtering.

"I care nothing, not I—say what you like; I've had worse losses in my time," he cried.

He plunged his right hand into his breast and drew out something.

"See, that, mate?" he said, and held it up under the glass chandelier.

It was a little curl of brown hair, tied across the middle with a piece of faded blue ribbon.

"See it?" he cried in a husky gurgle. "It's all I've got left in the world."

He held it up to the light and looked at it, and laughed until the glass pendants of the chandelier swung and jingled with the vibration of his voice.

"The gorse under the ling, eh? There you are then! *She* gave it me. Yes, though, on the night I sailed. My gough! The ruch and proud I was that night anyway! I was a homeless beggar, but I might have owned the stars, for, by God, I was walking on them going away."

He reeled again, and laughed as if in mockery of himself, and then said, "That's ten year ago, mate, and I've kep' it ever since. I have though, here in my breast, and it's druv out wuss things. When I've been far away foreign, and losing heart a bit, and down with the fever, maybe, in that ould hell, and never looking to see herself again, no, never, I've been touching it gentle and saying to myself, soft and low, like a sort of an angel's whisper, 'Nelly is with you, Davy. She isn't so very far away, boy; she's here for all.' And when I've been going into some dirt of a place that a dacent man shouldn't, it's been cutting at my ribs, same as a knife, and crying like mad, 'Hould hard, Davy; you can't take Nelly in theer?' When I've been hot it's been keeping me cool, and when I've been cold it's been keeping me warm, better till any comforter. D'ye see it, sir? We're ould comrades, it and me, the best that's going, and never no quarreling and no words neither. Ten years together, sir; blow high, blow low. But we're going to part at last."

Then he picked up the candle in his left hand, still holding the lock of hair in his right.

"Good-by, ould friend!" he cried, in a shrill voice, rolling his head to look at the curl, and holding it over the candle. "We're parting company to-night. I'm going where I can't take you along with me—I'm going to the divil. So long! S'long! I'll never strook you, nor smooth you, nor kiss you no more! S'long!"

He put the curl to his lips, holding it tremblingly between his great fingers and thumb. Then he clutched it in his palm, reeled a step backward, swung the candle about and dashed it on to the floor.

"I can't, I can't," he cried, "God A'mighty, I can't. It's Nelly—Nelly—my Nelly—my little Nell!"

The curl went back into his breast. He sank into a chair, covered his face with his hands, and wept aloud as little children do.

HALL CAINE

VII

When Mrs. Quiggin came down to breakfast next morning, a change both in her appearance and in her manner caught the eye and ear of Jenny Crow. Her fringe was combed back from her forehead, and her speech, even in the first salutation, gave a delicate hint of the broad Manx accent. "Ho, ho! what's this?" thought Jenny, and she had not long to wait for an answer.

An English waiter, who affected the ways of a French one, was fussing around with needless inquiries—*would Madame have this; would Madame do that?*—and when this person had scraped himself out of the room Mrs. Quiggin drew a long breath and said, "I don't think I care so very much for this sort of thing after all, Jenny."

"What sort of thing, Nelly?"

"Waiters and servants, and hotels and things," said Nelly.

"Really!" said Jenny.

"It's wonderful how much happier you are when you can be your own servant, and boil your own kettle and mash your own tea, and lay your own cloth, and clear away and wash up afterward."

"Do you say so, Nelly?"

"Deed I do, though, Jenny. There's some life in the like of that—seeing to yourself and such like. And what are the pleasures of towns and streets and hotels and servants, and such botherations to those of a sweet old farm that is all your own somewhere? And, to think—to think, Jenny, getting up in the summer morning before the sun itself, when the light is that cool dead gray, and the last stars are dying off, and the first birds are calling to their mates that are still asleep, and then going round to the cowhouse in the clear, crisp, ringing air, and startling the rabbits and the hares that are hopping about in the haggard—O! it's delightful!"

"Really now!" said Jenny.

"And then the men coming down stairs, half awake and yawning, in their shirt sleeves and their stocking feet, and pushing on their boots and clattering out to the stable, and shouting to the horses that are stamping in their stalls; and then you yoursef busy as Thop's wife laying the cups and saucers, and sending the boys to the well for water, and filling the big crock to the brim, and hanging the kettle on the hook, and setting somebody to blow the fire while the gorse flames and crackles, and bustling here and bustling there, and stirring yoursef terr'ble, and getting breakfast over, and starting everybody away to his work in the fields—aw, there's nothing like it in the world."

"And do *you* think that, Nelly?" said Jenny.

"Why, yes; why shouldn't I?" said Nelly.

"Well, well," said Jenny. "'There's nowt so queer as folk,' as they say in Manchester.

"What do you mean, Jenny Crow?"

"I fancy I see you," said Jenny, "bowling off to Balla—what d'ye call it?—and doing all that *by yourself.*"

"Oh!" said Nelly.

Mrs. Quiggin had begun to speak in a voice that was something between a shrill laugh and a cry, and she ended with a smothered gurgle, such as comes from the throat of a pea-hen. After breakfast Peggy Quine came chirping around with a hundred inquiries about the packing of luggage which was then proceeding, with a view to the carriage that had been ordered for eleven o'clock. Mrs. Quiggin betrayed only the most languid interest in these hurrying operations, and settled herself with her needlework in a chair near to Jenny Crow. Jenny watched her, and thought, "Now, wouldn't she jump at a good excuse for not going at all?"

Presently Mrs. Quiggin said, in a tone of well-acted unconcern, "And so you say that the poor man you tell me of is still loving his wife in spite of all she has done to him?"

"Yes, Nelly. All men are like that—more fools they," said Jenny.

Nelly's face brightened over the needles in her hand, and her parted lips seemed to whisper, "Bless them!" But in a note of delicious insincerity she only said aloud, "Not all, Jenny; surely not all."

"Yes, all," said Jenny, with emphasis. "Do you think I don't know the men better than you do?"

Nelly dropped her needles and raised her face. "Why, Jenny," she said, "however can that be?—you've never even been married."

"That's why, my dear," said Jenny.

Nelly laughed; then returning to the attack, she said, with a poor pretense at a yawn, "So you think a man may love a woman even after—after she has turned him out of doors, as you say?"

"Yes, but that isn't to say that he'll ever come back to her," said Jenny.

The needles dropped to the lap again. "No? Why shouldn't he then?"

"Why? Because men are never good at the bended knee business," said Jenny. "A man on his knees is ridiculous. It must be his legs that look so silly. If I had done anything to a man, and he went down on his knees to me, I would——"

"What, Jenny?"

Jenny lifted her skirt an inch or two, and showed a dainty foot swinging to and fro. "Kick him," she answered.

Nelly laughed again, and said, "And if you were a man, and a woman did so, what then?"

"Why lift her up and kiss her, and forgive her, of course," said Jenny.

Nelly tingled with delight, and burned to ask Jenny if she should not at least let Captain Davy know that she was leaving Douglas and going home. But being a true woman, she asked something else instead.

"So you think, Jenny," she said, "that your poor friend will never go back to his wife?"

"I'm sure he won't," said Jenny. "Didn't I tell you?" she added, straightening up.

"What?" said Nelly, with a quiver of alarm.

"That he's going back to sea," said Jenny.

"To sea!" cried Nelly, dropping her needles entirely. "Back to sea?" she said, in a shrill voice. "And without even saying 'good-by!'"

"Good-by to whom, my dear?" said Jenny. "To me?"

"To his wife, of course," said Nelly, huskily.

"Well, we don't know that, do we?" said Jenny. "And, besides, why should he?"

"If he doesn't he's a cruel, heartless, unfeeling, unforgiving monster," said Nelly.

And then Jenny burned in her turn to ask if Nelly herself had not intended to do as much by Captain Davy, but, being a true woman as well as her adversary, she found a crooked way to the plain question. "Is it at eleven," she said, "that the carriage is to come for you?"

Mrs. Quiggin had recovered herself in a moment, and then there was a delicate bout of thrust and parry. "I'm so sorry for your sake, Jenny," she said, in the old tone of delicious insincerity, "that the poor fellow is married."

"Gracious me, for my sake? Why?" said Jenny.

"I thought you were half in love with him, you know," said Nelly.

"Half?" cried Jenny. "I'm over head and ears in love with him."

"That's a pity," said Nelly; "for, of course, you'll give him up now that you know he has a wife."

"What of that? If he *has* a wife I have no husband—so it's as broad as it's long," said Jenny.

"Jenny!" cried Nelly.

"And, oh!" said Jenny, "there is one thing I didn't tell you. But you'll keep it secret? Promise me you'll keep it secret. I'm to meet him again by appointment this very night."

"But, Jenny!"

"Yes, in the garden of this house—by the waterfall at eight o'clock. I'll slip out after dinner in my cloak with the hood to it."

"Jenny Crow!"

"It's our last chance, it seems. The poor fellow sails at midnight, or tomorrow morning, or to-morrow night, or the next night, or sometime. So you see he's not going away without saying good-by to somebody. I couldn't help telling you, Nelly. It's nice to share a secret with a friend one can trust, and if he *is* another woman's husband—"

Nell had risen to her feet with her face aflame.

"But you mustn't do it," she cried. "It's shocking, it's horrible—common morality is against it."

Jenny looked wondrous grave. "That's it, you see," she said. "Common morality always *is* against everything that's nice and agreeable."

"I'm ashamed of you, Jenny Crow. I am; indeed, I am. I could never have believed it of you; indeed, I couldn't. And the man you speak of is no better than you are, and all his talk of loving the wife is hypocrisy and deceit; and the poor woman herself should know of it, and come down on you both and shame you—indeed, she should," cried Nelly, and she flounced out of the room in a fury.

Jenny watched her go and thought to herself. "She'll keep that appointment for me at eight o'clock to-night by the waterfall." Presently she heard Mrs. Quiggin with a servant of the hotel countermanding the order for the carriage at eleven, and engaging it instead for the extraordinary hour of nine at night. "She intends to keep it," thought Jenny.

"And now," she said, settling herself at the writing-table; "now for the *other* simpleton."

"Tell D. Q.," she wrote, addressing Lovibond; "that E. Q. goes home by carriage at nine o'clock to-night, and that you have appointed to meet her for a last farewell at eight by the waterfall in the gardens of Castle Mona. Then meet *me* on the pier at seven-thirty."

VIII

L ovibond received this message while sitting at breakfast, and he caught the idea of it in an instant. Since the supper of the night before he had been pestered by many misgivings, and troubled by some remorse. Capt'n Davy was bent on going away. Overwhelmed by a sense of what he took to be his dastardly conduct he was in that worst position of the man who can forgive neither himself nor the person he has injured. So much had Lovibond done for him by the fine scheme that had brought matters to such a pass. But having gone so far, Lovibond had found himself at a stand. His next step he could not see. Capt'n Davy must not be allowed to leave the island, but how to keep him from going away was a bewildering difficulty. To tell him the truth was impossible, and to concoct a further fable was beyond Lovibond's invention. And so it was that when Lovibond received the letter from Jenny Crow, he rose to the cue it offered like a drowning man to a life-buoy.

"Jealousy—the very thing!" he thought; and not until he was already in the thick of his enterprise as wizard of that passion did he realize that if it was an effectual instrument to his end it was also a cruel one.

He found Capt'n Davy in the midst of the final preparations for their journey. These consisted of the packing of clothes into trunks, bags, sacks, and hampers. On the floor of the sitting-room lay a various assortment of coats, waistcoats, trowsers, great-coats, billycock hats and sou'-westers, together with countless shirts and collars, scarfs and handkerchiefs. At Davy's order Willie Quarrie had gathered up the garments in armsful out of drawers and wardrobes, and heaped them at his feet for inspection. This process they were undergoing with a view to the selection of such as were suitable to the climate in which it was intended that they should be worn. The hour was 8.30 A.M., the "Snaefell" was announced to sail for Liverpool at nine.

But, as Lovibond entered the room, a scene of yet more primitive interest was actively proceeding. A waiter of the hotel was strutting across the floor and sputtering out protests against this unseemly use of the sitting-room. The person was the same who the night before had haunted Davy's elbow with his obsequious "Yes, sirs," "No, sirs," and "Beg pardon, sirs"; but the morning had brought him knowledge of Davy's penury, and with that wisdom had come impudence if not dignity.

"The ideal!" he cried. "Turnin' a 'otel drawrin'-room into a charwoman's laundry!"

"Make it a rag shop at once," said Davy, as he went on quietly with his work.

"A rag shop it is, and I'll 'ave no more of it," said the waiter loftily. "Who ever 'eard of such a thing?"

"No?" said Davy. "Well, well, now! Who'd have thought it? You never did? A rael Liverpool gentleman, eh? A reg'lar aristocrack out of Sawney Pope-street!"

"No, sir, but it's easy to see where *you* came from," said the waiter, with withering scorn.

"You say true, boy," said Davy, "but it's aisier still to see where you are going to. Ever seen the black man on the beach at all? No? Him with the performing birds? You know—jacks and ravens and owls and such like. Well, he's been wanting something like you this long time. Wouldn't trust, but he'd give twopence-halfpenny for you—and drinks all round. You'd make his fortune as a cockatoo."

The waiter in fury called downstairs for assistance, and when two of his fellow servants had arrived in the room they made some poor show of working their will by force. Then Davy paused from his work, scratched the under part of his chin with the nail of his forefinger, and said, "Friends, some of us four is interrupting the play, and they're wanting us at the pay box to give us back the fare. I'm thinking it's you's fellows—what do *you* say? They're longing for you downstairs—won't you go? No? you'll not though? Then where d'ye keep the slack of your trowsis?"

Saying this Davy rose to his feet, hitched his left hand into the collar of the first waiter, and his right into the depths under his coat tails, and ran him out of the room. Returning for the other two waiters he did much the same by each of them, and then came back with a look of awe, and said—

"My gough! they must have been Manxmen after all—they rowled downstairs as if they'd been all legs together."

Lovibond looked grave. "That's going too far, Capt'n," he said. "For your own sake it's risking too much."

"Risking too much?" said Davy. "There's only three of them."

The first bell rang on the steamer; it was quarter to nine o'clock. Willie Quarrie looked out at the window. The "Snaefell" was lying by the red pier in the harbor, getting up steam, and sending clouds of smoke over the old "Imperial." Cars were rattling up the quay, passengers were making for the gangways, and already the decks, fore and aft, were thronged with people.

"Come along, my lad; look slippy," cried Davy, "only two bells more, and three hampers still to pack. Tumble them in—here goes."

"Capt'n!" said Willie, still looking out.

"What?" said Davy.

"Don't cross by the ferry, Capt'n."

"Why not?"

"They're all waiting for you," said Willie, "every dirt of them all is waiting by the steps—there's Tommy Tubman, and Billy Balla-Slieau, and that wastrel of a churchwarden—yes, and there's ould Kennish—they're all there. Deng my buttons, all of them. They're thinking to crow over us, Capt'n. Don't cross by the ferry. Let me run for a car. Then we'll slip up by the bridge yonder, and down the quay like a mill race, and up to the gangway like smook, and abooard in a jiffy. That's it—yes, I'll be off immadient, and we'll bate the blackguards anyway."

Willie was seizing his cap to carry out his intention of going for a cab in order that his master might be spared the humiliation of passing through the line of false friends who had gathered at the ferry steps to see the last of him; but Davy shouted "Stop," and pointed to the hampers still unpacked.

"I'm broke," said he, "and what matter who knows it? Reminds me, sir," said Davy to Lovibond, "of Parson Cowan. The ould man lived up Andreas way, and after sarvice he'd be saying, 'Boys let's put a sight on the Methodees,' and they'd be taking a slieu round to the chapel door. Then as the people came out he'd be offering his snuff-boxes all about. 'William, how do? have a pinch?' 'Ah, Robbie, fine evening; take a sneeze?' 'Is that you, Tommy? I haven't another box in my clothes, but if you'll put your finger and thumb into my waistcoat pocket here, you'll find some dust.' Aw, yes, a reglar up-and-a-downer, Parson Cowan, as aisy, as aisy, and no pride at all. But he had his wakeness same as a common man, and it was the Plow Inn at Ramsey. One day he was going out of it middling full—not fit to walk the crank anyway—when who should be coming up the street from the court-house but the Bishop! It was Bishop—Bishop—chut, his name's gone at me—but no matter, glum as a gur-goyle anyway, and straight as a lamppost—a reglar steeple-up-your-back sort of a chap. Ould Mrs. Beatty saw him, and she lays a hould of Parson Cowan and starts awkisking him back into the house, and through into the parlor where the chiney cups is. 'You mustn't go out yet,' the ould woman was whispering. 'It's the Bishop. And him that sevare—it's shocking! He'll surspend you! And think what they'll be saying! A parson, too! Hush, sir hush! Don't spake! You'll be waiting till it's dark, and then going home with John in the bottom of the cart, and nice clane straw to lie on, and nobody knowing nothing.' But the ould man wouldn't listen. He drew hisself up on the ould woman tremenjous, and studdied hisself agen the door, and 'No,' says he; 'I'm drunk,' says he, 'God knows it,' says he, 'and for what man knows I don't care a damn—*I'll walk!*' Then away he went down the street past the Bishop, with his hat a-one side, and his hair all through-others, tacking a bit with romps in the fetlock joints, but driving on like mad."—

The second bell rang on the steamer. It was seven minutes to nine, and the last of the luggage was packed. On the floor there still lay a pile of clothing, which was to be left as oil for the wounded joints of the gentlemen who had been flung down stairs. Willie Quarrie bustled about to get the trunks and hampers to the ferry steps. Davy, who had been in his shirt-sleeves, drew on his coat, and Lovibond, who had been waiting twenty torturing minutes for some opportunity to begin, plunged into the business of his visit at last.

"So you're determined to go, Capt'n?" he said.

"I am," said Davy.

"No message for Mrs. Quiggin? Dare say I could find her at Castle Mona."

"No! Wait—yes—tell her—say I'm—if ever I—Chut! what's the odds? No, no message."

"Not even good-by, Capt'n?"

"She sent none to me—no."

"Not a word?"

"Not a word."

Davy was pawing up the carpet with the toe of his boot, and filling his pipe from his pouch.

"Going back to Callao, Capt'n?" said Lovibond.

"God knows, mate," said Davy. "I'm like the seeding grass, blown here and there, and the Lord knows where; but maybe I'll find land at last."

"Capt'n, about the money?—dy'e owe me any grudge about that?" said Lovibond.

"Lord-a-massy! Grudge, is it?" said Davy. "Aw, no, man, no. The money was my mischief. It's gone, and good luck to it."

"But if I could show you a way to get it all back again, Capt'n——"

"Chut! I wouldn't have it, and I wouldn't stay. But, matey, if you could show me how to get back. . . the money isn't the loss I'm. . . if I was as poor as ould Chalse-a-killey, and had to work my flesh. . . I'd stay if I could get back. . ."

The whistle sounded from the funnel of the "Snaefell," and the loud throbs of escaping steam echoed from the Head. Willie Quarrie ran in to say that the luggage was down at the ferry steps, and the ferryboat was coming over the harbor.

"Capt'n," said Lovibond, "she must have injured you badly——"

"Injured *me*?" said Davy. "Wish she had! I wouldn't go off to the world's end if that was all betwixt us."

"If she hasn't, Capt'n," said Lovibond, "you're putting her in the way of it."

"What?"

Davy was about to light his pipe, but he flung away the match.

"Have you never thought of it?" said Lovibond, "That when a husband deserts his wife like this he throws her in the way of—"

"Not Nelly, no," said Davy, promptly. "I'll lave *that* with her, anyway. Any other woman perhaps, but Nelly—never! She's as pure as new milk, and no beast milk neither. Nelly going wrong, eh? Well, well! I'd like to see the man that would. . . I may have treated her bad. . . but I'd like to see the man, I say. . ."

Then there was another shrieking whistle from the steamer. Willie Quarrie called up at the window and gesticulated wildly from the lawn outside.

"Coming, boy, coming," Davy shouted back, and looking at his watch, he said, "Four minutes and a half—time enough yet."

Then they left the hotel and moved toward the ferry steps. As they walked Davy begun to laugh. "Well, well!" he said, and he laughed again. "Aw, to think, to think!" he said, and he laughed once more. But with every fresh outbreak of his laughter the note of his voice lost freshness.

Lovibond saw his opportunity, and yet could not lay hold of it, so cruel at that moment seemed the only weapon that would be effectual. But Davy himself thrust in between him and his timid spirit. With another hollow laugh, as if half ashamed of keeping up the deception to the last, yet convinced that he alone could see through it, he said, "No news of the girl in the church, mate, eh? Gone home, I suppose?"

"Not yet," said Lovibond.

"No?" said Davy.

"The fact is—but you'll be secret?"

"Coorse."

"It isn't a thing I'd tell everybody—"

"What?"

"You see, if her husband has treated her like a brute, she's his wife, after all."

Davy drew up on the path. "What is it?" he said.

"I'm to meet her to-night, alone," said Lovibond.

"No!"

"Yes; in the grounds of Castle Mona, by the waterfall, after dark—at eight o'clock, in fact.

"Castle Mona—by the waterfall—eight o'clock—that's a—now, that must be a—"

Davy had lifted his pipe hand to give emphasis to the protest on his lips, when he stopped and laughed, and said, "Amazing thick, eh?"

"Why not," said Lovibond? "Who wouldn't be with a sweet woman like that? If the fool that's left her doesn't know her worth, so much the better for somebody else."

"Then you're for making it up there?" said Davy, clearing his throat.

"It'll not be my fault if I don't," said Lovibond. "I'm not one of the wise asses that talk big about God's law and man's law; and if I were, man's law has tied this sweet little woman to a brute, and God's law draws her to me—that's all."

"And she's willing, eh?" said Davy.

"Give her time, Capt'n," said Lovibond.

"But didn't you say she was loving this—this brute of a husband?" said Davy.

"Time, Capt'n, time," said Lovibond. "That will mend with time."

"And, manewhile, she's tellin' you all her secrets."

"I leave you to judge, Capt'n."

"After dark, you say—that's middling tidy to begin with, eh, mate—eh?"

Lovibond laughed: Capt'n Davy laughed. They laughed together.

Willie Quarrie, standing by the boat at the bottom of the steps, with the luggage piled up at the bow, shouted that there was not a minute to spare. The throbbing of the steam in the funnel had ceased, one of the two gangways had been run ashore, and the captain was on the bridge.

"Now, then, Capt'n," cried Willie.

But Davy did not hear. He was watching Lovibond's face with eyes of suspicion. Was the man fooling him? Did he know the secret?

"Good-by Capt'n," said Lovibond, taking Davy by the hand.

"Good-by, mate," said Davy, absently.

"Good luck to you and a second fortune," said Lovibond.

"Damn the fortune," said Davy, under his breath.

Then there was another whistle from the "Snaefell."

"Capt'n Davy! Capt'n Davy!" cried Willie Quarrie.

"Coming," answered Davy. But still he stood at the top of the ferry steps, holding Lovibond's hand, and looking into his face.

Then there came a loud voice from the bridge of the steamer— "Steam up!"

"Capt'n! Capt'n!" cried Willie from the bottom of the steps.

Davy dropped Lovibond's hand and turned to look across the harbor. "Too late," he said quietly.

"Not if you'll come quick, Capt'n. See, the last gangway is up yet," cried Willie.

"Too late," repeated Davy, more loudly.

"Just time to do it by the skin of your teeth, Capt'n," shouted the ferryman.

"Too late, I tell you," thundered Davy, sternly.

Meanwhile there was a great commotion on the other side of the harbor.

"Out of the way there!" "All ashore!" "Ready?" "Ready!" "Steam up— slow!" The last bell rang. The first stroke of nine was struck by the clock of the tower; one echoing blast came from the steam whistle, and the "Snaefell" began to move slowly from the quay. Then there were shouts from the deck and adieus from the shore. "Good-by!" "Good-by!" "Farewell, little Mona!" "Good-by, dear Elian Vannin!" Handkerchiefs waving on the steamer; handkerchiefs waving on the quay; seagulls wheeling over the stern; white churning water in the wake; flag down; and harbor empty.

"She's gone!"

Lovibond smiled behind a handkerchief, with which he pretended to wipe his big mustache. Willie Quarrie looked helplessly up the ferry steps. Davy gnashed his teeth at the top of them.

After a moment Davy said, "No matter; we can take the Irish packet at nine, and catch the Pacific boat at Belfast. Willie," he shouted, "put the luggage in the shed for the Belfast steamer. We'll sail to-night instead."

Then the three parted company, each with his own reflections.

"The Capt'n done that a-purpose," thought Willie.

"He'll keep my engagement for me at eight o'clock," thought Lovibond.

"I wouldn't have believed it of her if the Dempster himself had swore to it," thought Davy.

IX

At half-past seven that night the iron pier was a varied and animated scene. A band was playing a waltz on the circle at the end; young people were dancing, other young people of both sexes were promenading, lines of yet younger people, chiefly girls in short frocks, but with the wagging heads and sparkling eyes of one type of budding maidenhood, were skipping along arm-in-arm, singing snatches of the words set to the waltz, and beating a half-dancing time with an alternate scrape and stroke of the soles of their shoes upon the wood floor on which they walked. The odor of the brine came up from below and mingled with the whiffs of Mona Bouquet that swept after the young girls as they passed, and with the puffs of tobacco smoke that enveloped the young men as they dawdled on. Sometimes the revolving light of the lightship in the channel could be seen above the flash and flare of the pier lamps, and sometimes the dark water under foot gleamed and glinted between the open timbers of the pier pavement, and sometimes the deep rumble of the sea could be heard over the clash and clang of the pier band.

Lovibond was there, walking to and fro, feeling himself for the first time to be an old fellow among so many younger folks, watching the clock, counting the minutes, and scanning every female form that came alone with the crink-crank-crick through the round stile of the pay-gate.

Not until five minutes to eight did the right one appear, but she made up for the tardiness of her coming by the animation of her spirits.

"I couldn't get away sooner," whispered Jenny. "She watched me like a cat. She'll be out in the grounds by this time. It's delicious! But is he coming!"

"Trust him," said Lovibond.

"O, dear, what a meeting it will be!" said Jenny.

"I'd love to be there," said Lovibond.

"Umph! Would you? Two's company, three's none—you're just as well where you are," said Jenny.

"Better," said Lovibond.

The clock struck eight in the tower.

"Eight o'clock," said Lovibond, "They'll be flying at each other's eyes by this time."

"Eight o'clock, twenty seconds!" said Jenny. "And they'll be lying in each other's arms by now."

"Did she suspect?" said Lovibond.

"Of course she did!" said Jenny. "Did he?"

"Certainly!" said Lovibond.

"O dear, O dear!" said Jenny. "It's wonderful how far you can fool people when it's to their interest to be fooled."

"Wonderful!" said Lovibond.

They had walked to the end of the pier; the band was playing—

> *"Ben-my-chree!*
> *Sweet Ben-my-chree,*
> *I love but thee, sweet Mona."*

"So our little drama is over, eh?" said. Jenny.

"Yes; it's over," said Lovibond.

Jenny sighed; Lovibond sighed; they looked at each other and sighed together.

"And these good people have no further use for us," said Jenny.

"None," said Lovibond.

"Then I suppose we've no further use for each other?" moaned Jenny.

"Eh?" said Lovibond.

"Tut!" said Jenny, and she swung aside.

> *"Mona, sweet Mona,*
> *I love but thee, sweet Mona.'*

"There's only one thing I regret," said Lovibond, inclining his head toward Jenny's averted face.

"And pray, what's that?" said Jenny, without turning about.

"Didn't I tell you that Capt'n Davy had taken two berths in the Pacific steamer to the west coast?" said Lovibond.

"Well?" said Jenny.

"That's ninety pounds wasted," said Lovibond.

"*What* a pity!" sighed Jenny.

"Isn't it?" said Lovibond—his left hand was fumbling for her right.

"If she were any other woman, she might be glad to go still," said Jenny.

"And if he were any other man he would be proud to take her," said Lovibond.

"Some woman without kith or kin to miss her—" began Jenny.

"Yes, or some man without anybody in the world—" began Lovibond.

"Now, if it had been *my* case—" said Jenny, wearily.

"Or mine," said Lovibond, sadly.

Each drew a long breath.

"Do you know, if I disappeared tonight, there's not a soul—" said Jenny, sorrowfully.

"That's just my case, too," interrupted Lovibond.

"Ah!" they said together.

They looked into each other's eyes with a mournful expression, and sighed again. Also their hands touched as their arms hung by their sides.

"Ninety pounds! Did you say ninety? Two berths?" said Jenny. "What a shocking waste! Couldn't somebody else use them?"

"Just what I was thinking," said Lovibond; and he linked the lady's arm through his own.

"Hadn't you better get the tickets from Capt'n Davy, and—and give them to somebody before it is too late?" said Jenny.

"I've got them already—his boy Quarrie was keeping them," said Lovibond.

"How thoughtful of you, Jona—I mean, Mr. Lovi—"

"Je—Jen—"

"Ben-my-chree! Sweet Ben-my-chree, I love but thee—"

"O, Jonathan!" whispered Jenny.

"O, Jenny!" gasped Jonathan.

They were on the dark side of the round house; the band was playing behind them, the sea was rumbling in front; there was a shuffle of feet, a sudden rustle of a dress; the lady glanced to the right, the gentleman looked to the left, and then for a fraction of an instant they were locked in each other's arms.

"Will you go back with me, Jenny?"

"Well," whispered Jenny. "Just to keep the tickets from wasting—"

"Just that," whispered Lovibond.

Three quarters of an hour later they were sailing out of Douglas harbor on board the Irish packet that was to overtake the Pacific steamship next morning at Belfast. The lights of Castle Mona lay low on the water's edge, and from the iron pier as they passed came the faint sound of the music of the band:

"Mona, sweet Mona,
Fairest isle beneath the sky,
Mona, sweet Mona,
We bid thee now good-by."

X

The life that Davy had led that day-was infernal At the first shaft of Lovibond's insinuation against Mrs. Quiggin's fidelity he had turned sick at heart. "When he said it," Davy had thought, "the blood went from me like the tide out of the Ragged Mouth, where the ships lie wrecked and rotten."

He had baffled with his bemuddled brain, to recall the conversation he had held with his wife since his return home to marry her, and every innocent word she had uttered in jest had seemed guilty and foul. "You've been nothing but a fool, Davy," he told himself. "You've been tooken in."

Then he had reproached himself for his hasty judgment. "Hould hard, boy, hould hard; aisy for all, though, aisy, aisy!" He had remembered how modest his wife had been in the old days—how simple and how natural. "She was as pure as the mountain turf," he had thought, "and quiet extraordinary." Yet there was the ugly fact that she had appointed to meet a strange man in the gardens of Castle Mona, that night, alone. "Some charm is put on her—some charm or the like," he had thought again.

That had been the utmost and best he could make of it, and he had suffered the torments of the damned. During the earlier part of the day he had rambled through the town, drinking freely, and his face had been a piteous sight to see. Toward nightfall he had drifted past Castle Mona toward Onchan Head, and stretched himself on the beach before Derby Castle. There he had reviewed the case afresh, and asked himself what he ought to do.

"It's not for me to go sneaking after her," he had thought. "She's true, I'll swear to it. The man's lying. . . Very well, then, Davy, boy, don't you take rest till you're proving it."

The autumn day had begun to close in, and the first stars to come out. "Other women are like yonder," he had thought; "just common stars in the sky, where there's millions and millions of them. But Nelly is like the moon—the moon, bless her—"

At that thought Davy had leaped to his feet, in disgust of his own simplicity. "I'm a fool," he had muttered, "a reg'lar ould bleating billygoat; talking pieces of poethry to myself, like a stupid, gawky Tommy Big Eyes."

He had looked at his watch. It was a quarter to eight o'clock. Unconsciously he had begun to walk toward Castle Mona. "I'm not for misdoubting my wife, not me; but then a man may be over certain. I'll find out for myself; and if it's true, if she's there, if she meets him. . . Well, well, be aisy for all, Davy; be aisy, boy, be aisy! If the worst comes to the worst, and you've got to cut your stick, you'll be doing it without a heart-ache anyway. She'll not be worth it, and you'll be selling yourself to the Divil with a clane conscience. So it's all serene either way, Davy, my man, and here goes for it."

Meanwhile Mrs. Quiggin had been going through similar torments. "I don't blame *him*," she had thought. "It's that mischief-making huzzy. Why did I ask her? I wonder what in the world I ever saw in her. If I were not going away myself she should pack out of the house in the morning. The sly thing! How clever she thinks herself, too! But she'll be surprised when I come down on her. I'll watch her; she sha'n't escape me. And as for *him*—well, we'll see, Mr. David, we'll see!"

As the clock in the hall in Castle Mona was striking eight these good souls in these wise humors were making their several ways to the waterfall under the cliff, in the darkest part of the hotel grounds.

Davy got there first, going in by the gate at the Onchan end. It struck him with astonishment that Lovibond was not there already. "The man bragged of coming, but I don't see him," he thought. He felt half inclined to be wroth with Lovibond for daring to run the risk of being late. "I know someone who would have been early enough if he had been coming to meet with somebody," he thought.

Presently he saw a female form approaching from the thick darkness at the Douglas end of the house. It was a tall figure in a long cloak, with the hood drawn over the head. Through the opening of the cloak in front a light dress beneath gleamed and glinted in the brightening starlight. "It's herself," Davy muttered, under his breath. "She's like the silvery fir tree with her little dark head agen the sky. Trust me for knowing her! I'd be doing that if I was blind. Yes, would I though, if I was only the grass under her feet, and she walked on me. She's coming! My God, then, it's true! It's true, Davy! Hould hard, boy! She's a woman for all! She's here! She sees me! She thinks I'm the man?"

In the strange mood of the moment he was half sorry to take her by surprise.

Davy was right that Mrs. Quiggin saw him. While still in the shadow of the house she recognized his dark figure among the trees. "But he's alone," she thought. "Then the huzzy must have gone back to her room when I thought she slipped out at the porch. He's waiting for her. Should I wait, too? No! That he is there is enough. He sees me. He is coming. He thinks I am she. Umph! Now to astonish him!"

Thus thinking, and both trembling with rage and indignation, and both quivering with love and fear, the two came face to face.

But neither betrayed the least surprise.

"I'm sorry, ma'am, if I'm not the man——" faltered Davy.

"It's a pity, sir, if I'm not the woman——" stammered Nelly.

"Hope I don't interrupt any terterta-tie," continued Davy.

"I trust you won't allow *me*——" began Nelly.

And then, having launched these shafts of impotent irony in vain, they came to a stand with an uneasy feeling that something unlooked for was amiss.

"What d'ye mane, ma'am?" said Davy.

"What do *you* mean, sir?" said Nelly.

"I mane, that you're here to meet with a man," said Davy.

"I!" cried Nelly. "I? Did you say that I was here to meet——"

"Don't go to deny it, ma'am," said Davy.

"I do deny it," said Nelly. "And what's more, sir, I know why you are here. You are here to meet with a woman."

"Me! To meet with a woman! Me?" cried Davy.

"Oh, *you* needn't deny it, sir," said Nelly. "Your presence here is proof enough against you."

"And *your* presence here is proof enough agen you," said Davy.

"You had to meet her at eight," said Nelly.

"That's a reg'lar bluff, ma'am," said Davy, "for it was at eight you had to meet with *him*?

"How dare you say so?" cried Nelly.

"I had it from the man himself," said Davy.

"It's false, sir, for there *is* no man; but I had it from the woman," said Nelly.

"And did you believe her?" said Davy.

"Did *you* believe *him*?" said Nelly. "Were you simple enough to trust a man who told you that he was going to meet your own wife?"

"He wasn't for knowing it was my own wife," said Davy. "But were *you* simple enough to trust the woman who was telling you she was going to meet your own husband?"

"She didn't know it was my own husband," said Nelly. "But that wasn't the only thing she told me."

"And it wasn't the only thing *he* tould *me*." said Davy. "He tould me all your secrets—that your husband had deserted you because he was a brute and a blackguard."

"I have never said so," cried Nelly. "Who dares to say I have? I have never opened my lips to any living man against you. But you are measuring me by your own yard, sir; for you led *her* to believe that I was a cat and a shrew and a nagger, and a thankless wretch who ought to be put down by the law just as it puts down biting dogs."

"Now, begging you pardon, ma'am," said Davy; "but that's a damned lie, whoever made it."

After this burst there was a pause and a hush, and then Nelly said, "It's easy to say that when she isn't here to contradict you; but wait, sir, only wait."

"And it's aisy for you to say yonder," said Davy, "when he isn't come to deny it—but take your time, ma'am, take your time."

"Who is it?" said Nelly.

"No matter," said Davy.

"Who is the man," demanded Nelly.

"My friend Lovibond," answered Davy.

"Lovibond!" cried Nelly.

"The same," groaned Davy.

"Mr. Lovibond!" cried Nelly again.

"Aw—keep it up, ma'am; keep it up!" said Davy. "And, manewhile, if you plaze, who is the woman?"

"My friend Jenny Crow," said Nelly.

Then there was another pause.

"And did she tell you that I had agreed to meet her?" said Davy.

"She did," said Nelly. "And did *he* tell *you* that I had appointed to meet *him?*"

"Yes, did he," said Davy. "At eight o'clock, did she say?"

"Yes, eight o'clock," said Nelly. "Did *he* say eight?"

"He did," said Davy.

The loud voices of a moment before had suddenly dropped to broken whispers. Davy made a prolonged whistle.

"Stop," said he; "haven't you been in the habit of meeting him?"

"I have never seen him but once," said Nelly. "But haven't *you* been in the habit of meeting *her?*"

"Never set eyes on the little skute but twice altogether," said Davy. "But didn't he see you first in St. Thomas's, and didn't you speak with him on the shore—"

"I've never been in St. Thomas's in my life!" said Nelly. "But didn't you meet her first on the Head above Port Soderick, and to go to Laxey, and come home with her in the coach?"

"Not I," said Davy.

"Then the stories she told me of the Manx sailor were all imagination, were they?" said Nelly.

"And the yarns *he* told *me* of the girl in the church were all make-ups, eh?" said Davy.

"Dear me, what a pair of deceitful people!" said Nelly.

"My gough! what a couple of cuffers!" said Davy.

There was another pause, and then Davy began to laugh. First came a low gurgle like that of suppressed bubbles in a fountain, then a sharp, crackling breaker of sound, and then a long, deep roar of liberated mirth that seemed to shake and heave the whole man, and to convulse the very air around him.

Davy's laughter was contagious. As the truth began to dawn on her Mrs. Quiggin first chuckled, then tittered, then laughed outright; and at last her voice rose behind her husband's in clear trills of uncontrollable merriment.

Laughter was the good genie that drew their assundered hearts together. It broke down the barrier that divided them; it melted the frozen places where love might not pass. They could not resist it. Their anger fled before it like evil creatures of the night.

At the first sound of Davy's laughter something in Nelly's bosom seemed to whisper "He loves me still;" and at the first note of Nelly's, something clamored in Davy's breast, "She's mine, she's mine!" They turned toward each other in the darkness with a yearning cry.

"Nelly!" cried Davy, and he opened his arms to her.

"Davy!" cried Nelly, and she leaped to his embrace.

And so ended in laughter and kisses their little foolish comedy of love.

As soon as Davy had recovered his breath he said, with what gravity he could command, "Seems to me, Nelly Vauch, begging your pardon, darling, that we've been a couple of fools."

"Whoever could have believed it?" said Nelly.

"What does it mane at all, said Davy.

"It means," said Nelly, "that our good friends knew each other, and that he told her, and she told him, and that to bring us together again they played a trick on our jealousy."

"Then we *were* jealous?" said Davy.

"Why else are we here?" said Nelly.

"So you *did* come to see a man, after all?" said Davy.

"And *you* came to see a woman," said Nelly.

They had began to laugh again, and to walk to and fro about the lawn, arm-inarm and waist-to-waist, vowing that they would never part—no, never, never, never—and that nothing on earth should separate them, when they heard a step on the grass behind.

"Who's there?" said Davy.

And a voice from the darkness answered, "It's Willie Quarrie, Capt'n."

Davy caught his breath. "Lord-a-massy me!" said he. "I'd clane forgotten."

"So had I," said Nelly, with alarm.

"I was to have started back for Cajlao by the Belfast packet."

"And I was to have gone home by carriage."

"If you plaze, Capt'n," said Willie Quarrie, coming up. "I've been looking for you high and low—the pacquet's gone."

Davy drew a long breath of relief. "Good luck to her," said he, with a shout.

"And, if you plaze," said Willie, "Mr. Lovibond is gone with her."

"Good luck to *him*," said Davy.

"And Miss Crows has gone, too," said Willie.

"Good luck to her as well," said Davy; and Nelly whispered at his side, "There—what did I tell you?"

"And if you plaze, Capt'n," said Willie Quarrie, stammering nervously, "Mr. Lovibond, sir, he has borrowed our—our tickets and—and taken them away with him."

"He's welcome, boy, he's welcome," cried Davy, promptly. "We're going home instead. Home!" he said again—this time to Nelly, and in a tone of delight, as if the word rolled on his tongue like a lozenge—"that sounds better, doesn't it? Middling tidy, isn't it. Not so dusty, eh?"

"We'll never leave it again," said Nelly.

"Never!" said Davy. "Not for a Dempster's palace. Just a piece of a croft and a bit of a thatch cottage on the lea of ould Orrisdale, and we'll lie ashore and take the sun like the goats."

"That reminds me of something," whispered Nelly. "Listen! I've had a letter from father. It made me cry this morning, but it's all right now—Ballamooar is to let!"

"Ballamooar!" repeated Davy, but in another voice. "Aw, no, woman, no! And that reminds *me* of something."

"What is it," said Nelly.

"I should have been telling you first," said Davy, with downcast head, and in a tone of humiliation.

"Then what?" whispered Nelly.

"There's never no money at a dirty ould swiper that drinks and gambles everything. I'm on the ebby tide, Nelly, and my boat is on the rocks like a taypot. I'm broke, woman, I'm broke."

Nelly laughed lightly. "Do you say so?" she said with mock solemnity.

"It's only an ould shirt I'm bringing you to patch, Nelly," said Davy; "but here I am, what's left of me, to take me or lave me, and not much choice either ways."

"Then I take you, sir," said Nelly. "And as for the money," she whispered in a meaning voice, "I'll take Ballamooar myself and give you trust."

With a cry of joy Davy caught her to his breast and held her there as in a vice. "Then kiss me on it again and swear to it," he cried, "Again! Again! Don't be in a hurry woman! Aw, kissing is mortal hasty work! Take your time, girl! Once more! Shocking, is it? It's like the bags of the bees that we were stealing when we were boys! Another! Then half a one, and I'm done!"

Since they had spoken to Willie Quarrie they had given no further thought to him, when he stepped forward and said out of the darkness: "If you plaze, capt'n, Mr. Lovibond was telling me to give you this lether and this other thing," giving a letter and a book to Davy.

"Hould hard, though; what's doing now?" said Davy, turning them over in his hand.

"Let us go into the house and look," said Nelly.

But Davy had brought out his matchbox, and was striking a light. "Hould up my billycock, boy," said he; and in another moment Willie Quarrie was holding Davy's hat on end to shield from the breeze the burning match which Nelly held inside of it. Then Davy, bareheaded, proceeded to examine what Lovibond had sent him.

"A book tied up in a red tape, eh?" said Davy. "Must be the one he was writing in constant, morning and evening, telling hisself and God A'mighty what he was doing and wasn't doing, and where he was going to and when he was going to go. Aw, yes, he always kep' a diarrhea."

"A diary, Davy," said Nelly.

"Have it as you like, *Vauch*, and don't burn your little fingers," said Davy; and then he opened the letter, and with many interjections proceeded to read it.

"'Dear Captain. How can I ask you to forgive me for the trick I have played upon you? '(Forgive, is it?)' I have never had an appointment with the Manx lady; I have never had an intention of carrying her off from her husband; I have never seen her in church, and the story I have told you has been a lie from beginning to end.'"

Davy lifted his head and laughed.

"Another match, Willie," he cried. And while the boy was striking a fresh one Davy stamped out the burning end that Nelly dropped on to the grass, and said: "A lie! Well, it was an' it wasn't. A sort of a scriptural parable, eh?"

"Go on, Davy," said Nelly, impatiently, and Davy began again:

"'You know the object of that trick by this time' (Wouldn't trust), 'but you have been the victim of another' (Holy sailor!), 'to which I must also confess. In the gambling by which I won a large part of your money' (True for you!) 'I was not playing for my own hand. It was for one who wished to save you from yourself.' (Lord a massy!) 'That person was your wife' (Goodness me!), 'and all my earnings belong to her.' (Good thing, too!) 'They are deposited at Dumbell's in her name' (Right!), 'and—'"

"There—that will do," said Nelly, nervously.

"'And I send you the bank-book, together with the dock bonds, . . . which you transferred for Mrs. Quiggin's benefit. . . to the name. . . of her friend. . .'"

Davy's lusty voice died off to a whisper.

"What is that?" said Nelly, eagerly.

"Nothin'," said Davy, very thick about the throat; and he rammed the letter into his breeches' pocket and grabbed at his hat. As he did so, a paper slipped to the ground. Nelly caught it up and held it on the breezy side of the flickering match.

It was a note from Jenny Crow: "'You dear old goosy; your jealous little heart found out who the Manx sailor was, but your wise little poll never once suspected that Mr. Lovibond could be anything to anybody, although I must have told you twenty times in the old days of the sweetheart from whom I parted. Good thing, too. Glad you were so stupid, my dear, for by helping you to make up your quarrel we have contrived to patch up our own. Good-by! What lovely stories I told you! And how you liked them! We have borrowed your husband's berths for the Pacific steamer, and are going to have an Irish marriage tomorrow morning at Belfast—'"

"So they're a Co. consarn already," said Davy.

"'Good-by! Give your Manx sailor one kiss for me—'"

"Do it!" cried Davy. "Do it! What you've got to do only once you ought to do it well."

Then they became conscious that a smaller and dumpier figure was standing in the darkness by the side of Willie. It was Peggy Quine.

"Are you longing, Peggy?" Willie was saying in a voice of melancholy sympathy.

And Peggy was answering in a doleful tone, "Aw, yes, though—longing mortal."

Becoming conscious that the eyes of her mistress were on her, Peggy stepped out and said, "If you plaze, ma'am, the carriage is waiting this half-hour."

"Then send it away again," said Davy.

"But the boxes is packed, sir——"

"Send it away," repeated Davy.

"No, no," said Nelly; "we must go home to-night."

"To-morrow morning," shouted Davy, with a stamp of his foot and a laugh.

"But I have paid the bill," said Nelly, "and everything is arranged, and we are all ready."

"To-morrow morning," thundered Davy, with another stamp of the foot and a peal of laughter.

And Davy had his way.

THE END

A Note About the Author

Hall Caine (1853–1931) was a British author whose novels, short stories, poems, and criticism made him the most successful writer of his day. Born in Liverpool, Caine trained as an architectural draftsman before becoming a successful lecturer and theater critic. He then moved to London to live and work with the famous Pre-Raphaelite artist Dante Gabriel Rossetti, at which point Caine's literary career began in earnest. He went on to publish dozens of novels, stories, and plays, some of which would inspire important films from directors such as Alfred Hitchcock. Toward the end of Caine's career, he involved himself in local and international politics, undertaking humanitarian trips to Russia and advocating for American support for Allied forces during the Great War.

A Note from the Publisher

Spanning many genres, from non-fiction essays to literature classics to children's books and lyric poetry, Mint Edition books showcase the master works of our time in a modern new package. The text is freshly typeset, is clean and easy to read, and features a new note about the author in each volume. Many books also include exclusive new introductory material. Every book boasts a striking new cover, which makes it as appropriate for collecting as it is for gift giving. Mint Edition books are only printed when a reader orders them, so natural resources are not wasted. We're proud that our books are never manufactured in excess and exist only in the exact quantity they need to be read and enjoyed.

Discover more of your favorite classics with Bookfinity™.

- Track your reading with custom book lists.
- Get great book recommendations for your personalized Reader Type.
- Add reviews for your favorite books.
- AND MUCH MORE!

Visit **bookfinity.com** and take the fun Reader Type quiz to get started.

Enjoy our classic and modern companion pairings!

www.ingramcontent.com/pod-product-compliance
Lightning Source LLC
Chambersburg PA
CBHW020549130626
46552CB00007B/2818